Dear Reader,

You know how your first always has a special place in your heart? That's *The Mercenary* for me. I fell in love with Marc Savin the moment he sprang to life fourteen years ago. Fourteen years since *The Mercenary* was first published and T-FLAC began! Time flies when you're having fun. ☺ I'm *still* a little in love with Marc, even though he's been followed by twelve or thirteen other larger-than-life alpha T-FLAC operative heroes. He'll always be my first.

So when I was asked if I'd like to change anything before it went into reprint, I jumped at the chance, and was thrilled to see both Marc and Tory again.

While the basic story hasn't changed much from the original, what you will find is that I was able to expand Marc and Tory as characters in this updated version. I deeply explored what made them tick, and enhanced what they had to do to come together and, of course, how they eventually fall in love.

Rewriting *The Mercenary* was a lot like taking a perfectly good sweater, then pulling a thread here and there and trying to knit it all back together, only in a larger size than the original. Some things couldn't be changed and others changed so much it really was like writing a completely new book.

With that in mind, I welcome you back to a story that captured my heart from the very first. If you haven't read Marc and Tory's story before, you're in for a treat. If you have, I've added more excitement just for you, and hope you enjoy it even more than you did the first time!

Smooches,

*Cherry*

FEB - - 2008

# CHERRY ADAIR

## THE
# MERCENARY

Refreshed version of THE MERCENARY,
revised by author.

HQN™

ISBN-13: 978-0-373-77248-3
ISBN-10:        0-373-77248-3

THE MERCENARY

This is the revised text of the work that was first published by
Harlequin Enterprises Limited in 1994.

www.HQNBooks.com

**Printed in U.S.A.**

In loving memory of my mother, Petal Campbell,
who nurtured the woman I've become.

And Jean Reed, friend and mentor,
who nurtured the writer I've become.

Two strong, smart women whom I loved and admired.

I miss them both.

# THE
# MERCENARY

# *PROLOGUE*

THE RED SUV CAREENED up the mile-long driveway spraying dust and gravel and spooking the horses grazing by the fence. It had been a blistering day, and the dust generated by the approaching vehicle hung lazily in the hot early-evening air.

*Damn.*

Annoyed, Marc Savin narrowed his eyes. Knowing who his visitor was, he was tempted to go inside and lock the door. He swore again. He wasn't ready for company, even if it was a man he respected.

Alexander "Lynx" Stone, his ex-partner and friend. Marc hadn't seen him in two years. A good guy to have at your back—not that Marc needed backup anymore. He was retired. For good. Nothing Lynx could say would bring "Phantom" back.

It took everything out of a man when he was responsible for killing the woman he loved.

Marc kept his eyes on the plume of dust following the SUV and took a swig of beer. With his other hand he rubbed at the scar on his shoulder. The scar and the memories were two years old. The scar didn't hurt, but the memories still managed to keep him up nights.

The vehicle slid to a stop several yards away, and Alex unfolded his lean frame from the driver's seat. Slamming the door he rounded the back of his vehicle. "Hey," he said, unsmiling.

"Hey, yourself," Marc replied, not bothering to mask his annoyance. "Don't tell me, you were just in the neighborhood—"

"And decided to drop by," Alex finished with a faint smile that didn't reach his eyes.

Marc wondered how much Alex had guessed about his self-imposed exile, then wondered why he even cared. He took another drink.

"Nice place," Alex commented, glancing around at the ranch house, barn and fenced-in corral. A few quarter horses grazed in the pasture, while in another paddock a prize red bull lazily swatted at flies with his tail.

"I like it. What are you doing here?"

"It's Spider—"

*Ah, crap.* "No."

"Goddamn it, listen t—"

"Nothing you have to say is of any interest to me."

"The whole damn operation is going down in flames." This was Lynx talking now—not his friend Alex. "We found the three rogue agents."

That caught Marc's attention, in spite of his attempts to stay emotionally removed. "Yeah?"

"Curtis, Michaels…and Krista."

Marc was up and off the step before he thought about it, advancing on his friend as a red-hot rage fired his body. It had been so long since he'd felt anything other than apathetic that he startled himself with the leap of fury. "Bullshit!"

"Truth." Alex didn't back down from his rage, merely shot him an empathetic glance. "She was a double agent from the beginning—"

Marc didn't give him a chance to finish, simply connected his fist to Alex's jaw with a satisfying slam. Alex staggered back against his truck, rubbing his face ruefully. "Whoa! Don't kill the messenger."

"That's fucking crap, and you know it." Marc barely recognized the harsh sound of his own voice. Even while he was vaguely aware that he was overreacting, he reached over and grabbed a fistful of Alex's shirt, yanking him away from the vehicle. He landed another solid blow to the younger man's rockhard midsection.

"Would I shit you on something this important?" Alex expertly warded off his blows, refusing to fight back, which only fueled Marc's anger even more. Why was Alex lying about Krista? Red filmed his vision as he fought in defense of the woman he'd loved.

And murdered.

Alex finally joined in the fight, Marc's equal. "You don't have to be so effing stubborn." His friend swung.

Marc leaned into the punch, shifting before the fist connected to his nose. He hit Alex's solid belly, then hit him again, and took pleasure when his friend winced. "You're blaming an innocent woman, just because she's already dead."

Rubbing his stomach, Alex mumbled, "We followed a paper trail. Her signature was authenticated. The sat pictures were verified, as well. There's no doubt she was one of them. None."

Marc didn't know anything about papers or photos. He did know that Alex was merely humoring him as they exchanged blows. But, damn it, it felt good to be beating the crap out of someone. Too bad his friend had shown up when he'd been spoiling for a fight for months. He hadn't been invited, Marc though sourly, hitting him again, so he could damn well take his licks and then get lost.

Alex hit back, not holding his punches this time.

Good. Fine. Great.

Almost ten minutes passed before they staggered apart, exhausted and bloodied as the first star winked in the red-washed Montana sky.

"I didn't want to believe it, either, but the evidence is there, man." Alex exhaled, bent over at the waist. "She turned on her country, and on you. She was rotten, Marc." His mouth was bleeding, and he swiped at his lip with the back of his hand.

"Shut the hell up and get off my land. And don't fucking come back." If the news was true, then he'd spent the last two years of his life mourning a lie.

"Come with me to Marezzo," Alex countered. "We need you."

Needed him? What a joke. The information Alex had just shared about Krista changed everything, and yet the anger, pain and heartbreak flowed back into his system as if it had happened mere days ago.

Instead of years.

Two long damn years.

"They're dead, Marc. All of them."

"Shut up—"

"The royal family. The king and queen of Marezzo and their son and daughter. Executed. They didn't have a chance, with the information Spider had—"

Marc opened his mouth to say something, but found his throat had closed.

"Spider has the island, Marc. They've taken it over and God knows what they have planned. So go ahead and play cowboy if you want, but I'll be leaving tonight to stop them." Alex turned, not sparing Marc a glance as he walked away.

Rubbing his jaw, Marc stared after his friend. Alex still packed a hell of a punch. He waited, hoping Lynx would simply start the damn vehicle and leave. Instead, his friend reached into the open window and grabbed a thick manila envelope from the front seat.

"Read it and weep, you stubborn bastard." Alex threw it onto the wide porch. He rounded the vehicle and opened the door, then climbed in. "And try to sleep at night, thinking about what those butchers are getting away with."

It wasn't that Marc didn't want to. It wasn't that he even had a choice. Simple truth was, he'd be useless on a mission. Finding out that he'd been sleeping with, no, he admitted brutally, in love with, the enemy, solidified his belief. But could he, in good conscience, send his partner off to that island alone?

"Can't do it."

Something in his tone must have gotten through to his partner, because Alex looked down at his bruised knuckles grasping the steering wheel and studied them for an inordinate amount of time. When he finally spoke, his voice was tight. "Then tell me what the hell's going on—why have you refused missions for the last two years?"

"I was in the business for almost half my damn life. Half my life fighting other people's wars. I wanted out." It wasn't all a lie, but it wasn't all the truth, either. It would have to do. "Take care of yourself," Marc muttered, embarrassed by the emotion that had crept into his voice. "Don't be a goddamn fool over there."

"You've got my word on that." Alex's brilliant green eyes glowed in the lights from the dash. "Just promise me one thing."

"Yeah?"

"I screw up, pal, you come get me."

"Get going."

"Promise?"

"Will you leave if I do?"

"You have my word on it."

"For what that's worth. Okay, you got it, buddy."

Alex pressed his advantage. "I could do with some company."

Marc shook his head at his friend's persistence. "It's good to want things."

Alex hesitated then started the engine. "You know where to find me."

Yeah. He knew. Marc watched the SUV tear back down the gravel road like a bat out of hell. Alex drove the same way he attacked life. Full throttle.

He'd be back.

Marc returned to the top step of the porch as night stole over the ranch bringing with it a kind of peace he was learning to love. A horse nickered as the dust settled. The envelope Alex had left was behind him, but he never once turned to look at it.

It took him four days before he worked up the courage to open it.

Three days later word came that Alexander Stone was dead.

# CHAPTER ONE

NERVOUS PERSPIRATION prickled her skin.

Even though she couldn't hear breathing other than her own, her heightened sense of fear let her know she wasn't alone. Someone was watching her. Victoria Jones lay very still, eyes closed, heart pounding an uneven tattoo beneath her sore ribs.

Needing a few moments to orientate herself she tried to keep her breathing steady. A log flaring in the fireplace. There hadn't been a fire when she'd come in. But now she felt its heat and saw the dancing orange light through her eyelids.

To still her panic she counted to a hundred and twenty, then added another fifty for good measure, then slowly opened her eyes. The library was dim, but flickering firelight illuminated the lower half of the man sitting in the shadows across the room. Boots, long, jean-clad legs...the rest of him disappeared into darkness and shadow.

Heart lodged in her throat, she struggled to sit up. She'd accidentally fallen asleep, and now she was groggy and disoriented and at a distinct disadvantage.

The fact that the man wasn't saying anything intimidated her and made her feel defensive and automatically in the wrong. But she could be overreacting. Fear and exhaustion had taken up permanent residence in her body.

Her hair had come loose and floated around her shoulders and down her back as she swung her feet to the floor. Searching with her toes for her shoes, she tried with one hand to tame her hair back into its customary bun.

The man, and Tory knew he was Marc Savin even though he had yet to say a word, observed her without comment, increasing her unease. Still, her grandmother's strict teachings came to the fore and she said in a prim, polite voice, "I'm sorry. I must have fallen asleep."

Giving up on her hair, she pushed her feet all the way into her low heels and stood, despite her shaky knees. Piercing the darkness to gauge his reaction to her uninvited presence in his home, Tory felt marginally more in control with her shoes on. The silence stretched uncomfortably. He wasn't going to make this easy for her.

Why should he? He didn't even know her. Fidgeting, she realized that it was silly actually, standing or sitting, barefoot or not, the amount of intimidation radiating from him was all consuming. Tory had no clue how to deal with such a…a…presence.

The men she normally encountered in her day-to-day life were academics. Intelligent, cultured and extremely…low-key. Meek. But not Savin. She was fairly sure he didn't have a meek bone in his impressive body. Which was precisely why she was there.

"What happened?" he asked lazily. "Miss the exit for the Holiday Inn?"

His rough, deep voice startled her. His mockery added to her misery, and she waited for him to throw her out of his home. Not that she was going. She was a woman on a mission, she reminded herself, adding a little starch to her spine.

"I have jet lag. I didn't realize…" She tugged self-consciously at the hem of her jacket. "I didn't realize you'd be so long…." The man who'd let her in—reluctantly—had said his boss would be "right in." That had been—she glanced subtly at her watch—four hours ago.

"Did we have an appointment?"

"Um… No. We didn't. I'm Victoria Jones." She held her ground while a flush of heat betrayed her. His presence was larger than life and seemed to fill the room with a pulsing sensuality that made her extremely uncomfortable.

"And?" Marc said drily. He'd found that out by checking the driver's license in her purse. Her name meant nothing to him. When he'd bent to retrieve the tote from the floor beside her he'd gotten a lungful of a floral fragrance that had teased at his dormant libido. Ridiculous, of course. Even in the dim light, he knew this repressed-looking mouse wasn't his type at all.

The name and San Diego address on her license didn't reveal much. But what *was* mildly interesting was how hard she was trying to pretend she didn't have a cast on her left arm. It was barely visible beneath her sleeve, but its bulk was hard to miss.

He flipped on the light to get a better look at her. She looked like a throwback to the eighties, dressed as she was in a butt-ugly and unflattering business suit. Navy. The jacket boxy, the skirt neither tight nor loose. The hemline hitting just below the knee. Her sensible black shoes were polished and sported a modest heel. Christ, from the neck down she looked like a freaking stereotypical librarian.

Marc concentrated on her unattractive clothing, and kept his attention away from her soft mouth, and the mile of uncooperative dark hair she was trying, unsuccessfully, to cram back into a bun at her nape with one hand.

"Whatever you're selling, I don't need," he jabbed to see the spark of reaction. "Unless you're here about an overdue library fine?"

Her cheekbones flamed, but she didn't drop her gaze. Maybe not a mouse, then, he reevaluated, wondering just who in the hell she was. He'd never met her before, he was sure, but there was something vaguely familiar around the eyes....

Could her skin possibly be as soft as it appeared? It was pale, silky and looked as though it tasted like cream. Damn it, he needed to get laid. Soon.

"Snap it up, would you? I've had a bitch of a day. I'm cold, tired and hungry, and you're standing in the way of a hot shower and a meal."

"Are you Marcus Savin?"

"The one and only." He didn't bother to conceal his annoyance as he stepped from the shadows into the circle of light.

Tory blinked. In a flash she tried to take him in. Her world slowed its spin—a peculiar, terrifying feeling. Dread tightened her throat. Marc Savin wasn't anything like the man she'd envisioned.

He was about twenty years younger than she'd anticipated. And taller. Taller and broader, and disconcertingly male. His hair was thick and dark and tied back, revealing a winking diamond—a diamond!—in one ear. Good grief. His jeans were old and faded, the cream-colored fisherman's-knit sweater he wore looked soft and well-worn. The sweater was the only soft thing about him, she thought, mouth dry.

He looked like someone who'd stepped out of the pages of a magazine. What the casual yet well-dressed, brooding predatory male wore. Her eyes met his. Gray. Not the soft warm gray of a kitten or the comforting gray of a favorite blanket. His eyes were the cold, icy-pale gray of the sky just before a frost, the bleak soulless gray of bare tree branches frozen for all time. Tory shivered despite the blazing fire.

She could sense dismissal coming. Straightening her spine she stepped forward onto the thick Persian carpet between them, her hand outstretched. "Mr. Savin, I'm—"

"You've already told me who you are, Miss Jones. I just don't know what you're doing here."

For a moment her hand stayed poised in midair until she realized he had no intention of taking it. Her arm dropped to her side, and she flattened her damp palm against her thigh. Despite all the hours of rehearsal on the plane coming here, she was suddenly tongue-tied.

She knew what she must look like—an exhausted woman, with mussed dark hair and wrinkled clothes. She absently touched her face where the cushion had left an indentation on her cheek and forced herself not to fuss with her clothing. Her injured arm throbbed. But not for a moment was she going to let him see just how terrified she was. Girding herself, she tilted her chin and met his stare.

His gaze raked her body from head to toe. His eyes narrowed when he noticed the cast on her arm, and everything inside her froze as he asked grimly, "How did that happen?" She'd thought her sleeve covered the blasted thing.

"I fell." Into a wall. Unadulterated fear made her go icy cold all over. *Don't think about it. Don't think about it. Do not think about it.*

"Take off your jacket." He didn't move, but his words felt sinister.

She gave him a startled look while her heart pounded beneath her rib cage like a trapped animal. "What on earth for?"

"Because I say so."

"I'm a guest in your home, Mr. Savin. I won't be bullie—"

"Guest? Guests are invited. Don't make me strip it off for you. I'm too tired for games."

He was unyielding. As much as she hated obeying, Tory choked down her pride and shrugged off the jacket. It hadn't been easy getting the fiberglass into the sleeve, and it wasn't any easier getting that arm out. Bunching her jacket against her body, she held up her arm, shooting him a fulminating glare. Which might have been effective on some level if she hadn't felt her chin wobble.

She would *not* cry in front of him. She gritted her teeth. "Satisfied?"

"Far from it." His eyes took in the grubby cast showing beneath the edge of her white cotton sleeve, then scanned her face. It took every ounce of willpower she possessed not to touch any of the bruises she'd so carefully covered with foundation to make sure he couldn't detect them.

A muscle clenched in his jaw. "Who did this to you?"

"I told you. I fell." Often and hard. Oh, God. He was going to know she was lying through her teeth. She was lousy at it, and he seemed to be able to see directly into her brain with those pale, unamused X-ray eyes of his. Tory felt the heat in her cheeks get hotter and her gaze skittered back to the pattern on the carpet before she forced herself to meet his eyes.

"Let me put it this way, Miss Jones. I'll ask the questions. All you have to do is supply truthful answers. If I don't like what I hear, you'll be out of here so damned fast your head will spin. Got it? What happened to your arm?"

Tory licked her dry lips. "I was mugged at the airport."

"No abusive boyfriend or husband following you?"

Hateful man. "I'm not married."

His lips twitched. "Now why doesn't that surprise me?"

Tory tried to make her arm inconspicuous and bent to pick up her purse from the floor where it had fallen. Her mouth was dry and perspiration beaded on her skin. She was so tired of being scared. And he scared her to death. There was just…so much of him.

His hair, as dark as her own, was tied back in a short ponytail and the diamond stud flashed in one ear. His scuffed cowboy boots were set apart, his arms loose at his sides. He didn't look like a spy or a mercenary. Not that she'd had any idea what one looked like, but surely not like a cross between a *GQ* model and a predatory animal.

Obviously not impressed by what he was seeing, he said, "What can I do for you, Miss Jones? It must be something compelling to get you to stand here when you'd rather be anywhere else." His eyes shifted to the indented cushions on the sofa behind her and then narrowed on her face.

Victoria had never had a man look at her like that. It was disconcerting. She shrugged back into her jacket, despising herself for almost asking his permission to do so. But she didn't ask, and he made no comment as she buttoned the serviceable navy serge up to her throat.

The wind sounded mournful as it whipped the bare tree branches and rattled the window. The perfect setting for the nightmare she found herself living. Jerking her gaze away from the night sky, she turned back to him.

It didn't matter whether she liked him or not. Whether he scared her or not. She was here for one thing, and one thing only. "I need your help."

"Why should I help you?" He asked over his shoulder as he strolled to the built-in bar across the room and poured himself a drink. "I don't know you."

"May I have a drink, too, please?"

His shoulders tightened before he said in an amused voice, "Sure. You've already slept on my couch. What'll it be?"

She supposed that he had every right to his irritation. "Whatever you're having, I don't want to be a bother, really." She walked over to the French doors and rested her hand on the icy pane.

It had started snowing. The snow looked pretty illuminated by the lights from inside the house, soft, white. But snow was another unknown. She shivered. Already unnerved by too many weeks of the scary and the unfamiliar, Tory gritted her teeth and turned back into the room.

It was warmed by the blazing fire in the hearth, which caused reflections of dancing amber light from the highly polished dark-wood floor and the smooth surfaces of the two black leather sofas that flanked it. Wall-to-wall mahogany bookcases rose to twelve-foot ceilings. Victoria moved from the door to trail one hand across the tempting bookbindings before casting an anxious glance at the man across the room.

Having counted all the books on the left-hand wall after she'd arrived hours ago, she was about to start on the right when he came up behind her. She almost jumped out of her skin as he handed her a glass. The touch of his warm fingers across hers made her breath catch.

Too close, was her panicked reaction to his nearness. Much too close. She sidestepped, almost falling over her own feet in her haste to put a decent amount of space between them. She could feel the heat of his large body coming off him in waves. The smell of him, male and far too sexy, made her suck in a breath of surprise.

He scowled. "You okay?"

Tory's sheltered life hadn't in any way prepared her for him. It hadn't prepared her for anything else she'd experienced in the past few weeks, either. As Grammy used to say, What didn't kill you would make you stronger. She hoped.

Nodding, she realized he was waiting for a verbal response and choked out, "I'm perfectly fine, thank you." Oh, Lord. She sounded just like her grandmother.

He gave her an undecipherable glance, and she stayed where she was even though every intelligent cell in her brain was telling her to run. Fast and far away from Marc Savin. The safest tactic was to find a fault, an Achilles' heel to focus on that might make him less intimidating. Her gaze hunted for just such a flaw.

What man wore a stupid ponytail? If his hair had been loose, it would probably touch his broad shoulders. At least it was clean. And shiny. And silky looking. Her plan wasn't working too well. Oh, good Lord. Get a grip.

His snug jeans outlined the bulge… Oh my God, Victoria Francis! Stop looking at his…at his— She took a long drink. The liquid was room temperature and wet and for an instant felt very soothing as it slid down her throat—until it burned her esophagus like fire.

His expression was impassive as she gasped for breath and the whiskey fumes made her eyes water and her throat close up. It took every ounce of her control not to cough.

She shot a poisonous glare at his back as he saun-tered across the room.

"Next time," he told her unsympathetically, "ask for water." Jesus, she was a throwback. An anomaly. One small shy, question mark. The clothes. The hair. The skittish demeanor. None of which added up in this day and age; it made her almost intriguing. There was some-thing vaguely familiar about her. Especially around the eyes, but he knew he'd never met her before. *Her* he would have remembered.

While there was less ranch work in winter, he'd still put in a long day. Tired and hungry, Marc dropped down on the leather sofa opposite her and stretched out his legs, the drink balanced on his belly. He settled one arm behind his head and watched her.

Christ, she was skittish. Her eyes slid away from his, then back. Her arrogant little nose tilted.

The mugging story was bogus. There were many ways to detect a liar, even a good one. Marc hadn't needed to see the pupils of her enormous green eyes dilate, nor did he have to hear the way her speech raced when she was telling him she'd been mugged.

Victoria Jones was a lousy liar.

Besides the broken arm she had contusions on her slender neck, and more bruises beneath the light appli-cation of makeup on her otherwise unblemished face. He was almost intrigued enough to dig deeper.

Almost.

"You know my brother." She moved cautiously to the other end of the sofa and sat on the very edge, pulling her skirt down lower over her calves. When she leaned forward to put her glass on the coffee table, she exposed the vulnerable ridge of her collarbone below the lacy edge of her collar. "Alex—Alexander Stone."

Alexander Stone and Victoria *Jones?* He narrowed his eyes fractionally. "I don't know anyone by that name. Sorry, honey. Try again."

"Lynx," she said tightly. "You know him as Lynx. He was sent on a mission to Marezzo seven months ago." She straightened and stared at him. "I'm his sister." Her jaw tightened and something flashed in her green eyes. "And don't say you don't know him. He told me all about you."

Marc just stared at her.

"I know, for example—" Tory kept her eyes fixed on a point behind his left ear "—that the organization you work for is an elite unit. A cloaked counterterrorist force beyond even the CIA. A highly secret group called T-FLAC. Terrorist Force Logistical Assault Command." She licked her bottom lip. "I know there are members of your team who have infiltrated any number of foreign governments and military organizations all over the world."

A small triumphant smile curved her mouth when she detected the slightest tensing of his broad, impressive shoulders. His eyes bored into hers like burning ice. "Who the hell are you, lady?"

She tried, God help her, she really tried, to say her name, but she was so terrified her lips barely moved. Her eyes darted about the room, looking for help; but of course they were alone. With a sinking heart she suddenly realized that other than Marc Savin's people, no one knew she was here. He could do anything to her and probably would. He shook her and Tory's teeth chattered. "My brother—"

"Would sure as hell not turn rogue and give away so much information dead or alive. Try again, green eyes. I'll give you two seconds to tell me who sent you, and then—"

"Your code name is Phantom," she said quickly, her skin going hot, then cold and clammy. Victoria smoothed her jacket down with a shaking hand. "My brother is alive and not well in Marezzo, Mr. Macho Spymaster. That's fact. The only reason I know all this is because—"

The eyes. *Alex's* eyes. But—"He didn't have any relatives."

"Try again, Mr. Savin." She echoed his words. "I'm sitting right here. I'm his twin and I'm very much alive." Tension radiated off her body. "And don't talk about him in the past tense. Alex is alive."

Damn, was it possible? Was it even conceivable that Lynx was alive? Of course the canny Lynx would have kept a sister under wraps, hence the name difference. He was normally a closemouthed bastard and would have known she'd be an easy target for anyone with a grudge. Then again, she could be anybody.

With familiar green eyes and access to him?

Despite the evidence, Marc was still skeptical. If his enemies wanted to get close to him, sending in someone like Victoria Jones was a clever maneuver. She sure as shit didn't look like an enemy operative. In fact she looked the exact opposite of dangerous.

But then, as he well knew, there was danger, and then there was danger. "How do I know you're his sister?"

"Don't be ridiculous! Why would I be here if I wasn't?" she shot back, and her eyes, so much like her brother's, flashed again. "He has a birthmark on his right leg shaped like a half-moon." She obviously didn't realize how much she exposed as she furiously yanked up her skirt to bare a slender thigh. A pink birthmark, shaped like a half-moon, marred the smooth skin under her panty hose.

"It's a moot point, isn't it?" Marc retorted, deceptively relaxed as she shoved her skirt back into place. "He died while he was on vacation, I believe." And if the son of a bitch wasn't dead, he would be when Marc found him. He thought of what he'd been through in the last six months. Only Lynx could have blown their cover like this. Marc's mind was racing with the ramifications of Lynx's betrayal. Had Lynx come to the ranch to lure Phantom into a trap?

"He was captured while he was on a mission," she insisted. "You let him go there alone and you had better get him out."

"I saw his body seven months ago."

She flinched. "I beg your pardon, but I saw him alive two weeks ago." Marc saw the muscles work in her throat. "He's been imprisoned for almost seven months. They— they've tortured him."

She lifted huge green eyes to his, and Marc found himself drawn into their anguished depths. He cursed under his breath. It wasn't possible. He'd seen the body. It had been burned beyond recognition, but the dental records... Hell, it had been Alexander Stone. He was sure of it.

Damn, but he was sick of this business. Every time he got close to someone, he lost them. Lynx had been the last straw. He was getting too damn old for this shit. Thank God he wasn't involved any more.

His head shot up as he suddenly realized what she'd said. His eyes narrowed.

"What the hell do you mean, you saw him?"

## CHAPTER TWO

MY GOD, COULD IT BE TRUE? Had this mousy woman with her blushes and accusing big green eyes done what a team of experienced T-FLAC operatives should have done, but hadn't? Had she actually gone to Marezzo, by herself for God's sake—and made contact with Lynx? A man the entire T-FLAC organization swore was *dead*?

Improbable.

Impossible.

Bullshit.

Then what the hell was she doing in Nowhere, Montana in the middle of freaking winter?

He'd been out of the counterterrorist business for almost three years, but he still had enemies. "Who really sent you?"

"No one."

Right. Who the hell would send *her* to him? Made no frigging sense. A stacked redhead in a skimpy outfit would have made more sense if someone wanted to send in a Trojan horse. But a mousy brunette sporting bruises, a broken arm and dressed like a repressed librarian? He'd never be that desperate.

The fact that he was trying to picture what she looked like underneath that yardage of navy serge was beside the point. A frisson of sexual heat curled in his belly, shocking the living hell out of him.

*Whoa.*

While he gave her motivation some thought Marc poured himself another drink. Something he'd been careful about not doing in the last year or so. Great. He'd known this woman for barely half an hour and she was already driving him to drink. The whiskey tasted fine going down. Better than fine. Smooth. He finished the two fingers and was tempted to go back for more. He'd done a helluva lot of drinking after... After. But anesthetizing himself with well-aged scotch wasn't the answer.

Fuck. He barely knew what the question was anymore.

She flinched when his empty heavy-bottomed crystal glass hit the end table. It sounded like a pistol shot in the momentary quietness. He was fine with silence. In fact he liked it a hell of a lot better than listening to inane chatter. Unfortunately his guest didn't hold the same sentiment.

Her throat worked, but her eyes, mossy green, and direct, met his. "I went there to find my brother."

Yeah. So she'd just said. Not only was it illogical, but it sure as shit didn't bear *repeating*. Goddamn it! He pressed the bridge of his nose between his thumb and forefinger. "Marezzo isn't exactly a vacation paradise, honey. You can't just go waltzing over there as if you were taking a little holiday." His blood ran cold at the thought of a civilian on that volatile little island in the Tyrrhenian Sea. It had been a hot spot for tangos for years.

"I wasn't *on* holiday." She glared at him as if *he* were the one who'd lost his freaking mind. "I didn't have a choice as to location. Alex is there, so that's where I went."

Honest to God, Marc thought as he observed the thudding of her pulse at the base of her slender throat, she sounded rational. Scared out of her mind, but rational. She appeared to be the real—if ten years out of step—deal. Christ. He wanted Alexander Stone to be alive. A part of him almost believed it. Almost. Even if it was only for a few minutes.

But wishing was for fools.

He was going to have to let her down gently, she looked like a crier. He ran his hand around the back of his neck. He'd rather face twenty heavily armed tangos alone than deal with a crying woman. She was watching him as warily as a mongoose watched a snake. Did she ever relax? She was stiff as a board, and sitting on the very edge of the middle cushion of the sofa opposite him. Her feet were placed precisely together, her knees locked.

If Ragno had Lynx—Fuck. If Ragno had Lynx, then Lynx truly was dead. Nobody had ever managed to extricate themselves from Ragno's sadistic handiwork. Which was why Alex's body had been so damned hard to ID.

"Look," he started. Fast and expedient? Or slow and sympathetic? He voted for fast. He'd get someone to escort her to the closest hotel and be left the hell alone. "I'm sorry to burst your bubble, but—"

"He's being held by a terrorist or a *group* of terrorists called 'Spider'."

The hair on the back of his neck lifted. *Spider*. Ragno's merry band of tangos *was* based in Italy. Last known address—Marezzo. Shit.

"It's a group." The terrorists had taken control of the island some time ago. Tourists were tolerated. Barely. "I know damn well that going over there with a broken arm like a little lame bird wouldn't even get a sympathetic glance from the people you're talking about. They'd kill you in a frigging heartbeat if you so much as looked as though you were going to—" *Interfere*. "Cause trouble."

Had Spider…? No. They'd do more than break a bone or two. He dismissed the idea out of hand that she'd actually had a close encounter with her brother's captors. She wouldn't be sitting here if that were the case.

Besides, she didn't look as though she were capable of saying "boo" let alone causing any trouble with a terrorist cell that was currently holding the number one spot on T-FLAC's most-wanted list.

"Well, it wasn't my first choice, I can assure you. But you people weren't doing anything to help Alex, so I had to." Her expressive eyes burned with hostility when he did no more than cross one ankle over his knee. "Are you going to sit there berating me all night, or are you going to go into action any time soon?"

Keeping his expression impassive, Marc bit back a reluctant chuckle, the first small ember of amusement he'd felt in years. "I'm out of the action business, honey. Sorry."

Way the hell out of the action business. Two years, seven months, and counting. He was a fucking rancher now. The only weapon he needed to carry was a factory load, model .350 Magnum scoped hunting air rifle. Rancher. Not an operative. He was done saving the world. He'd sucked at it, and he had written *beendet*, *fini*, *klaar* to the whole counterterrorist business once and for all.

He was no fucking hero. And he was fine with that.

"Then I suggest you take a drink, or swallow a vitamin, or do whatever it is you spy types do to get motivated," she told him crossly. "Because I'm not leaving here until you agree to—"

"Do you ever stop talking?"

"I talk when I'm nervous."

"You must be nervous a lot."

She swallowed. "I am."

It wasn't that he didn't believe what she was saying. He did. He believed it all right. He just couldn't wrap his brain around it. Was it possible that Alex really was alive? After all this time?

After he'd seen his body? What there was left of it…. Bile rose in the back of Marc's throat as he vividly recalled the day they'd brought what was left of Lynx to T-FLAC HQ in a heavy black body bag for ID.

What they'd done to him on the island hadn't been pretty. His friend hadn't died easy.

"The Spiders are serious people, green eyes, and Marezzo is no place for little Miss Muffet."

Up went the chin, baring the long pale line of her throat. "Well, after my visit, I can certainly see why tourism has gone down. I had my wallet stolen. Twice."

Was she fricking *joking?* At first he thought she might be, but when he looked at her, he saw that she was quite serious. She was ticked off because her wallet had been lifted. In Marezzo? She was damned fortunate she was still in one piece.

Or was she?

She'd yet to mention the cast she was trying valiantly to hide beneath the sleeve of her ugly suit jacket. Or the bruises she'd done a piss-poor job of covering with makeup. On the other hand he couldn't imagine the tangos would've let her walk away with a few broken bones and a handful of bruises. That wasn't the way they made their point.

Alex's skin had been black and crisp, charred almost beyond recognition. His friend had also been brutally tortured. Marc rubbed the flat of his hand across the heavy pressure of guilt in his chest. Alex's fingers, toes and dick had been amputated. Antemortem.

Spiders were the baddest of the bad guys.

"You're damn lucky those bastards only took your wallet," he told her, wanting another drink. He ignored the half-filled bottle across the room winking at him in the firelight.

The dying fire bathed her face in a rosy glow that made her look a whole lot more appealing. That or the two glasses of whiskey were kicking in. That or three years of abstinence. Take your pick, asshole, he told himself sourly. Any or all of the above.

Appealing. But not to him, of course. Her type of woman drove him nuts. Her naiveté irritated. He wished to God she'd cover her thighs. Her skin was ivory pale and he'd bet his prize bull it was silky and just too damned touchable.

He ran his gaze from her scraped-back dark hair, across her smooth cheeks, shied away from the surprising sensuality of her mouth, skimmed down her throat and traveled all the way to her sensible shoes. She jumped as if he'd used a cattle prod, jerking the skirt down as far as she could. Her face turned scarlet.

He scowled. "You're twenty-six years old, for God's sake. You should've known better than to go to an infamous world hot spot and stick your nose into something you couldn't even begin to understand. What's next? A hike through the Afghan desert or a scenic cruise to the Caspian Sea with a day trip to Chechnya? Christ, lady, maybe you should read a newspaper or watch a little CNN before you go flitting around the world."

"I wasn't flitting, I was investigat— How do you know how old I am?"

"I took a wild guess that you and your twin were close to the same age," he said drily, pushing off the sofa. He was a good six feet away from her, but she blinked several times as he crossed in front of her heading for the bar.

Nervous? Good. She had just cause. He turned his back on her and strode across the room. It wasn't so much the booze he needed, it was movement. Action. There wasn't enough damn room in the den. Not for the two of them anyway.

He could smell her. Female. Flowers. Innocence.

Fuck it.

He needed to be outside, under the open sky. He glanced at the window. Still snowing. Great. Just great.

It suited his mood perfectly. Cold. Dark. Depressing. He felt trapped here in his house, his castle, with *her.* Marc wasn't sure why, but he felt…besieged. As if the enemy had breached the walls of his sanctuary.

Carrying the half-empty bottle and ignoring his moronic analogy—hell, she was all of five feet, five inches tall, and probably weighed in at under a hundred and twenty pounds—he moved back to the fireplace. Putting the bottle down on the table he crouched to toss in another log. He flicked her a glance as the new log burst into an explosion of sparks.

"You want me to go and get him, is that it?" he asked mildly as he straightened.

Not him. No way in hell. But *someone.*

T-FLAC HQ was a hop, skip and jump away from the ranch. One call, and he'd—*they'd*—have a team wheels up, and en route to Italy, and the island of Marezzo.

"Of course. Would I be here if I wanted him to linger in that horrible country? You're the only one who can bring him back."

"Lady, your brother was—" *My best friend. A damn fine T-FLAC operative. One more fucking rock in this suitcase of guilt I've been lugging around.*

"*Is.*"

That deceptively soft exterior held a will of steel. "If," he continued without pause, "he was alive, I assure you, I'd know it." *I'll know one way or the other before you wake up in the morning,* he thought grimly. And it would probably be a good idea not to picture this woman sleepy-eyed and naked amidst crumpled sheets at this time.

"Well he is, and you didn't," she countered reasonably. She rose, the coffee table between them. He'd never known a female over the age of thirteen who blushed as much as this one did. And the suit—the suit was too damn big. Too old-fashioned. Too—hell—everything was wrong with it. He'd never met a woman who was so clueless about how to dress flatteringly. It wasn't a suit so much as a sack and for some inexplicable reason, it made him wonder what she was hiding under it.

Her legs were long, and from what he could see of them, well shaped, with incredibly delicate ankles. Luckily he'd always been a breast man so her legs didn't have much effect on him. Not much. Had any man seen her naked? Probably not.

The lush mouth said come here, and the green eyes shouted go to hell. *Please,* he added with an inward smile. He stood his ground as she circumvented the coffee table between them.

She tilted her head back to look up at him. Marc felt the shock of her small hand on his arm right through his thick sweater. He wanted to shake her off. But her touch was as light as a butterfly, and seductively gentle. She smelled like heaven.

He needed to get a grip. Shake her off and make that call. The sooner the better.

"They have him in Pescarna," she said quietly, a tremor in her husky voice. "It's a little fishing village on the southwest side of the island. He's in really bad…" Her short nails dug into his arm through the wool, and she swallowed hard, her eyes suddenly swimming with tears. "They've hurt him. Badly. He—he didn't even recognize me."

Her fingers tightened on his arm. "Please. Help me."

"No." He was going to get help for *Alex*.

For a moment there was silence as Tory stared up at him. "No? You're saying no? Despite the fact that he's your best friend and partner, you won't go in and rescue him?" Her jaw ached with fury and frustration.

Marc stepped away from her and leaned an elbow against the oak mantel, looking as relaxed as a cat. The silly diamond winked in his ear. She'd like to twist that lobe, as Grammy had done to her when she'd been naughty, until he stopped being so macho and actually *listened* to what she was telling him.

"It's nice to know you have such a good command of the English language, Miss Jones. You got it in one. Your brother was/is a good operative, and like all good operatives, he went in knowing the odds and the consequences."

Her heart was beating much too fast. He couldn't refuse, he just could not refuse. "But you thought he was dead. Now that you know that he isn't—"

"Makes absolutely no difference. I told you. I don't work for T-FLAC any longer. I don't have access to any intel. And even if I did—"

"What kind of man are you? They're *torturing* him. How can you just stand there so complacently and not care? Even if you *don't* work for them anymore, you still have the experience, the skills, the contacts, don't you?"

One moment he was completely relaxed, the next he

was right in her face. "'No' is a complete sentence. Want me to spell it out for you?"

A tidal wave of panic threatened to drown her. Her knees locked and her insides did somersaults at his nearness. Lord he was big. Big and mean looking, long hair and earring notwithstanding. The muscles in her stomach constricted as if she could at least draw that small part of herself away from the overwhelming menace of him. His whisky-scented breath was hot on her face, animosity radiated off him like a force field. She'd give everything she owned to have that much confidence. That much power.

Not particularly brave or adventurous in the first place, she'd been running on sheer nerves and bravado for days.

"This ranch is the only thing that keeps me marginally sane and reminds me I'm still part of the human race," he told her grimly. "Just because your brother gave you my name does not give you the right to barge into my home and demand anything. Got that?"

He was so close, Tory could see the pale squint lines beside his eyes and smell the faint scent of soap on his skin. The fiery heat of his body, so close to hers, made her dizzy. She flinched, her trembling fingers touching her throat as he looked down at her, his eyes narrowed and hard.

When she remained mute he said softly, "I spent almost half my life in hell so that people like you can sleep safe and sound in their beds at night. I'm just not interested anymore in saving a damsel in distress, whatever her problem."

His words stunned her. Alex had called this man the

best friend he'd ever had. "You heartless son of a— I can't believe that anyone could be so—*so unfeeling.* Alex thinks of you as a close friend."

"In this business I don't have any friends."

"I can certainly see why. With a friend like you, who needs enemies?" Okay. That was probably *not* the way to get this cold-eyed man motivated.

Tory felt the wild thundering of her pulse and swallowed hard. Her eyes focused on the subtle plaid of the wallpaper and for several seconds she counted the horizontal lines. She wasn't up to his sparring weight. Not tonight at any rate. She knew she wouldn't be up to his weight even if she *were* in tip-top physical condition. Which she wasn't at the moment. She was beyond exhausted, out of her mind with worry. And flat-out terrified.

None of that mattered. She couldn't fail Alex. No matter how tough, how mean, how unmotivated this man was, she had to get through to him. Tonight.

This was the only shot she had.

"That leaves me with only two choices."

"I can assure you, I don't want to know what they are. Time for you to leave. I'll give you directions to the local Motel 6 if you like."

"One," she said firmly, ignoring him as best she could. "I can go back again, and try to find him by myself…"

His laugh sounded rusty and not terribly amused. "How'd that work for you the first time around? If you could have gotten him out, you wouldn't be here now."

"Two," she continued as if he hadn't spoken. "I can go into town and talk to the nice people at the local newspaper." She looked at him with guileless eyes. "There is a newspaper in Brandon, isn't there? I'm sure they'd love to have the scoop. Do the townspeople have any idea you're a mercenary?"

Tory had heard the threat coming out of her mouth— she just couldn't believe she'd actually had the guts to make it. Her heart pounded and her palms became damp when he stepped closer.

She refused to be bullied, even though he was well over six feet, and he towered over her. His unshaven jaw was taut with fury in a face that was too masculine, too hard to ever be handsome. His nose was an aristocratic slash between dark brows that were drawn inward. He glared at her, a muscle jumping in his cheek as he stopped a hairbreadth in front of her.

She swallowed sickly, refusing to back up. *Don't show fear,* she told herself grimly. *Do not show this man one inch of fear.*

The diamond earring glittered as he shifted to lift her chin with his finger. "You," he said with lethal softness, "are either very brave or very stupid."

Tory gulped. Her eyes felt bone-dry as she forced herself to hold his gaze. The sound of her racing heart was loud in her ears.

Still tilting her face up he said flatly, "No one knows that you're here, do they, Miss Jones?" Before she could even formulate a reply he continued. "Did it ever occur to that agile little brain of yours that you might know just too damn much?" His fingers tightened around her jaw. "That if I am who you think I am, I can't let you leave here?"

His grip stretched Tory's skin painfully across her cheekbones. Her body was paralyzed as he held her gaze. "No one would know if you disappeared from the face of the earth, now would they? So if the 'local newspaper' needed a story, and someone just happened to find a mutilated body down by the river— Oh, for God's sake. Don't faint—"

He caught her as her eyes rolled and she slumped forward. The cast on her arm banged into the coal scuttle and he winced as he swung her up in his arms and strode over to the sofa, where he gently laid her down.

He was a bastard. An asshole, dickhead son of a bitch. He'd never mistreated a woman in his life. And doing so now, to *her,* proved just how damned low he'd sunk. When she didn't open her eyes, he moved the arm in the cast out of the way, and started undoing the little pearl buttons of her blouse. Her skin *was* silky smooth and warm.

He jerked his hand back when the back of his fingers accidentally—swear to God *accidentally*—brushed the plump curve of her breast.

Not boxy at all.

Miss Jones was all lush curves and hidden valleys. Marc dragged his hand away, and kept his attention on her face.

His words had only partially been a bluff.

She knew more than was good for her.

He stopped unbuttoning at the third button. Her breathing was just fine. He was surprised, however, at how pleasurable it was to touch her skin, and be sitting close enough to inhale the flowery fragrance of her. She wasn't plain at all, he thought watching the gentle rise and fall of her chest beneath the lace-collared white blouse. She had regained consciousness, but kept very still, eyes closed. Playing possum. Again.

He'd never scared anyone into a swoon before. He found himself not liking that she was his first. She was pale and limp. He didn't like that he felt sympathetic, either. That wasn't who he was. Who he used to be, hell…

"Unless you want me to administer CPR, open your eyes and take a swig of this." He wanted her awake and aware when he booted her out the door. Then he was going to make that call.

He wasn't going to tell her and get her hopes up, or listen to her opinion on how the retrieval—please God, there was one—was to go down. She could suffer, preferably in silence, for a few more hours. When he got news, she'd be the first to know.

If there was even the smallest, most remote chance that Alex was alive, Marc was going to call in the cavalry to go bring him home.

Her lids fluttered before she fixed her big green eyes on his face. "You are a hateful man."

"So I've been told." Marc picked up the barely tasted glass of whiskey she'd set on the table earlier. He ran his hand under the back of her head to lift her so she could drink. Bad mistake. Bad, bad, *bad* fucking mistake touching her.

Her hair was thick, and felt like cool silk tangled between his callused fingers. "Drink."

She parted her lips and took dainty sips of whiskey.

Long dark strands of her hair escaped in thick skeins from the bun-thing at her nape to tumble down her back as she sat up, taking the glass from him.

He had an image—a fleeting, foolish image—of burying his face in the waist-length strands. Of feeling the cool silk draped across his naked thighs...

"You're very literal, aren't you?" He absently wiped a drop of amber liquid off her bottom lip with his thumb. She stared up at him, unblinking, as he rose and set the empty glass back on the table.

Victoria Jones was a dangerous woman.

"Actually," she said in a small voice, frowning as she rubbed her fingers across her forehead, "I'm pretty much a coward."

"You could have fooled me." Marc's tone was dry.

"Really?" She looked ridiculously pleased as she swung her legs to the floor, feeling around for her shoes, which she must have lost when she'd keeled into his arms. When she couldn't find them she settled one foot on top of the other. "Well, I might be a chicken but I don't usually faint like that. Sorry."

She tried to wrangle a yard of silken hair back into a tight little bun. Wasn't working. Not one-handed, and he sure as hell wasn't going to offer to help. Her hair had a life of its own as it unfurled like ribbons of black satin around her shoulders. *Her* touching it turned him on.

"Leave it."

Her hand dropped to her lap.

Refilling his glass—hell, what was one more drink at this point?—he quietly watched her. The silence built and built and he could tell by the stiffness of her shoulders that she was ready to break, which was fine with him. He would give her directions to the motel in the next town and be ecstatic to see the back of her.

Her chin wobbled.

Marc ground his teeth. Tell her you're going to have a team sent…. No. A few more hours of worry wouldn't kill her.

A tear welled and ran down the side of her nose; another followed. Marc scowled. The fact that she didn't utter a sound made the tears more poignant. He jammed his fingers into the back pockets of his jeans and glared into the leaping flames. In his mind's eye he saw her shoulders heaving, but when he turned to look, she was as still as a statue. Her lips were moving in a silent litany, which Marc realized was counting. He'd noticed her doing the same thing earlier. It must help her calm down.

It sure as hell wasn't helping him, and he was up to two thousand eighty-six.

He was either going to kiss her or kill her and since neither was an option, it looked as though he was going to have a hell of a hangover tomorrow. He drew in a deep breath. Two thousand eighty-seven, two thousand…

## CHAPTER THREE

"HE'S—" THERE WAS A CATCH in her voice as she turned to face him. Her soft, pale mouth trembled as she whispered helplessly, "He's all I have. Please. Please, help me."

Marc felt the ice around his heart melt a little. He looked down at her glossy hair. When he didn't answer she wiped the tears off her face and turned her head to look out the window, obviously trying to compose herself. Her back was ramrod straight.

Damn it, didn't she realize that her blouse was undone? His eyes were drawn to the slender wedge of pale skin he could see reflected in the window—skin that looked so soft and smooth and...defenseless. Marc squeezed the bridge of his nose.

"Put that blanket around you or do up your blouse," he said, more gruffly than he'd have liked as he forced himself to concentrate on her face. He hated the life he'd left behind. Hated the thought of Alex's fate. Mostly, he hated himself for caving in. "Tell me everything."

Flushing, Tory buttoned her blouse and pulled the blanket around her shoulders, as well.

She sank back with a wince and blew a breath upward to clear a tendril of hair from her eyes. Covered to her knees by the mohair blanket, she looked like an orphan rescued from a storm. With every movement she made, more and more hair slithered loose from the coil at the back of her head.

"Where do you want me to start?"

Marc came and sat on the coffee table, facing her, their knees almost touching. "Start at the beginning and don't stop until I tell you."

"I have—*had*," she corrected, "a condo in San Diego. I always kept a room for Alex. He'd come once in a while and stay for a few days in between…assignments. Not as often as I liked, but he did stay a few times a year." She shrugged out of the blanket and he saw the pink mark where it had scratched her throat. The blanket settled around her hips as she fiddled with her hair. She used the waist-length strands like worry beads and Marc absently filed that information away. Better than wondering what those glossy strands would feel like trailing across his body.

"He used to send me a letter—mailed to a post office box in Mission Valley before each assignment. I was to keep it until he came and got it. I'd pick up the letter, take it home and wait for him. He'd come back and burn the letter. I never read any of them—not until the last one."

"What made this time different?" He leaned over and tugged at the blanket until it covered her knees to his satisfaction. Surprised, she looked at him, then continued softly: "He always gave me a time frame. Ninety days. I was supposed to wait for ninety days after he was due back, before I opened it. A week after he was due back I had this awful feeling—I just knew that something had gone drastically wrong…."

"What made you think he wouldn't be back?" Marc asked. "He came back late from assignments before. We all do. Can't be helped. It isn't like these things ever run on a fixed timetable."

"We have a…connection." She looked him straight in the eye. "A telepathic connection, if you will."

Marc couldn't negate what she'd said. T-FLAC had a special psi branch in fact, and he'd witnessed some amazing things while he'd been in the field. But he'd known Alexander Stone for six or seven years—and never seen any sign of him having any psychic ability. "So you packed your bags and went off on a little vacation to look for him? Is that what he told you to do in the letter?

"He told me where his last assignment was and told me to contact you if he wasn't back by the end of the month. And I didn't go on a 'little vacation.' I called you. You were gone. Indefinitely, they said. I couldn't wait. Alex was being hurt, and he was calling me. I went."

"Calling you? So the bad guys could trace the call and find *you?* I don't think so."

"Telepathically. I don't expect you to understand." Looking grim, she said urgently, "I knew he was in trouble. I had absolutely no idea when or if you would be back. For all I knew, you were with him."

Marc winced. Direct hit. He should have been with Lynx, then maybe things wouldn't have gone so wrong.

"I sold my condo and cashed in some other investments. I had no way of knowing how long it would take to get him out. I wanted all my resources liquid. Then I flew to Rome and from there I rented a boat and went to Marezzo."

Marc got up and started pacing again. "And you waltzed in and asked someone where your brother was?"

"Nobody asked me anything. I looked like a tourist. The pickpockets treated me like a tourist. I carried a camera and I did some sightseeing. And I did find my brother. Which," she said hotly, "is more than I can say for you."

Marc's temper flared. She was annoying as hell. But she was right. His people had shipped Alex Stone's body home. He'd done a cursory inspection and believed Lynx was in that body bag. He grabbed the phone, punched a series of numbers and waited. After rapping out a string of numbers, he held the line again. Tory sat stiffly, her face devoid of expression as she listened to his short commands.

"We have a code five on Marezzo," he said into the phone. "Who've we got? Yeah, lousy timing. I'll be coming myself. I'll take care at this end. I'll leave the transportation and ordnance to you." He looked at her assessingly and frowned. "I'm bringing someone with me. A woman. Expect us tomorrow at 0900."

"Surely you didn't mean..." Tory went white. "Oh, no! I can't go with you."

"I don't have a choice." Marc slammed down the phone and resumed his pacing. "You're the one who can communicate with him. If you're not with me, I might not be able to find him." If Lynx was alive—and that was a big fucking *if*—they might have moved him from his last known location. *If* what she said was true, and *if* she had some sort of psychic connection then he'd use it to expedite the search.

There were a shitload of *ifs*.

"Of course you will." She sounded panicked. "You're a spy. You do this kind of thing all the time. It's your job. You don't need me to slow you down." She held up her arm. "I have a broken arm. I can't go running around chasing the bad guys."

"Lady, that's your brother over there. If I say I need you, I need you. If I say go, you go. If I say jump, you ask how high. Got that?"

Her pupils dilated and she swallowed convulsively. "I don't do well under pressure. I'm a bookkeeper. Not Mata Hari. I work for an auto-parts store because I don't even like the pressure of tax time."

"You know what Will Rogers said. 'We can't all be heroes—someone has to sit on the curb and clap as we go by.'"

"I can clap for you from here."

"You're going."

"I could wait for you in Rome," she begged desperately.

"You're coming with me to Marezzo."

"I'll fall apart." Tory caught his wrist and stared up at him with pleading eyes. "Oh, please. Believe me. Taking me with you will be the worst mistake. I'll draw you a map of where they're holding Alex. You'll have no problem finding it. Really. Give me a pen and I'll show you—"

"Listen to me," Marc said slowly. "The last thing I want to do is haul your butt over there. But I don't seem to have a choice. Without your telepathic ability, I'm not sure I'll be able to find your brother." *Not in time, anyway.* "For all we know, they've moved him. You're going to Marezzo."

He didn't say that she was his insurance. If she was anything like Krista, he would give her no opportunity to set him up. Ninety percent of him believed her story. But he was listening to the all-important ten percent that told him to watch his back. Keep your enemies close. Victoria Jones was going to be right by his side whether she wanted to be or not. He gave her a cold look. "Unless you were bullshitting me about this telepathy bit?"

"No, that's the truth." Her shoulders slumped. "Don't say I didn't warn you, though, when I cower instead of attack."

"Nobody will be attacking anybody. We go in, find Alex and get the hell out." He'd get the job done. In, out. Clean and simple.

"Don't say I didn't try to warn you," she said weakly. "I just know you'll be sorry."

MARC WAS SORRY. Sorry he'd forced her to come, and sorrier still that they were on this stinking fishing boat from hell.

He was especially sorry she'd spent the first three hours puking her guts out over the side of the boat, mostly because he wanted to join her. The waves crashed into the side of the forty-foot hunk of wood until he was sure they'd have to swim the next hundred miles. She retched again, and his gut knotted in sympathy. Salt spray shot twenty feet in the air, soaking everything in sight, including her. He'd tried to keep her down in the relative warmth of the cabin, but the smell of fish had been so overpowering, even he hadn't been able to stomach it.

Tory dry-heaved over the side. Her stomach hurt, her arm throbbed, and she hated Marc Savin more with each passing moment. The man was relentless. He couldn't say she hadn't warned him.

"This really gives you a thrill, doesn't it, you bastard?" At the rough sound of Marc's voice, Tory raised her head weakly from the railing to glare at him. In case he hadn't noticed, she was *not* having a thrill a minute. But he wasn't talking to her. He was smiling that hateful smile and talking to the fisherman who was steering this death trap out to the open sea. Her head flopped back as her stomach heaved again and she groaned.

She was never stepping foot on anything smaller than a cruise ship ever again, she thought just before her stomach muscles cramped.

*"Certo!"* Angelo exclaimed with gusto, the muscles in his massive arms bulging with the strain of controlling the wheel. "Look at those waves, my friend. It makes us remember who is boss, no?"

Tory glanced up at the dark sky instead of at the mountainous waves beating the hull of the boat. A bright moon shone down, illuminating the glistening deck.

To the east a thick bank of clouds moved swiftly toward them.

"It makes me think you've used this damn cover too long," Marc told the other man. For all he knew she'd fallen overboard hours ago, she thought crossly. "Time you got back in the field, my friend. You're having just too damned much fun—I'd hate to see a trained T-FLAC operative lost to the sea. How soon till we get there?"

Angelo looked down at the waterproof watch on his massive wrist. "Give or take, 0500. The storm will cover you, but you're going to have to swim the last couple of hundred feet to the beach. You sure she'll make it?"

*She* wasn't sure she'd make it, Tory thought, holding tightly to the railing as Marc walked toward her, his body and long legs adjusting to the rocking of the deck.

"She'll make it if I make it," he said grimly, checking the plastic bag he'd wrapped around her cast to be sure it was still watertight. He handed her the canteen and told her to rinse her mouth out.

Gulping the water, Victoria shot him a furious look when he took it away and handed her a stick of gum.

"I don't chew gum," she said primly. "It isn't ladylike."

"Neither is puking your guts out." Marc unwrapped a piece and stuck it in her mouth. "Chew."

She glared at him from bleary eyes. "Remind me never to agree to go anywhere with you." Her jaw worked the gum. The flavor of mint bursting on her tongue was a blessing.

Marc suppressed a grin. "Another invitation isn't likely to come up. Can you make it for about forty more minutes?"

"What's the alternative?"

He pushed her dripping hair out of her eyes and laughed. "You could always swim."

"How far is it?" She looked serious. He supposed that now wasn't the time to let her know that she would be getting her wish. An enormous wave broke against the side and she let out a little shriek as hundreds of gallons of water crashed over them. Marc held on to the rail and pulled her against his chest as the wave foamed at their feet.

The wind whipped her hair into his face. It smelled of baby shampoo. "That was close." Burying his nose in the wet, fragrant mass he tightened his arms around her narrow waist.

Her voice, muffled by his yellow slicker, vibrated against his chest. "I don't even like this kind of adventure in a movie. I can't remember what it's like to be dry." Her bright eyes peered up at him. "And I think I swallowed my gum."

Marc chuckled and she pushed at his chest. "You're enjoying this, aren't you?"

Another wave crashed on deck a few feet away and he used it as an excuse to pull her closer. She fit rather well against him, despite the bulky slicker encasing her. "We spies just live for adventure." The corners of his mouth tilted in a reluctant grin.

Marc saw the pulse beat in her throat. Her dark lashes were spiky, her long hair slicked back, exposing a bruise and a bump on her forehead. She'd regained a little color and her lips were a pale petal pink.

My God, he thought in amazement. She's gorgeous.

She was still staring up at him, her arms wrapped around his waist as he dropped his mouth to hers.

Tory pushed him away with both hands against his chest. "Are you out of your *mind?*"

"Apparently."

"Were you trying to *kiss* me?" she asked with unflattering disgust.

"Hey, you two!"

Tory flushed, stepping away from Marc as Angelo shouted again. "Land ho!"

She looked over the side of the heaving boat. "Land ho—where?" All she could see in any direction were mountains of churning gray water beneath hills of black clouds.

She gripped the slick railing with one hand as Marc and Angelo gathered their things together. Angelo helped Marc shrug into the A.L.I.C.E. pack and then handed him several mysteriously wrapped packages, which Marc tucked into his belt.

He stripped off the slicker and bundled it into another pouch clipped to his belt. His jeans were black with water and the heavy cable-knit sweater sagged as he slipped off his shoes and used the laces to tie those to his belt, too.

Tory gave him a wary look as he made his way barefoot across the tilted deck toward her. Her lips still throbbed from anticipating that kiss. She could almost imagine her heated body sizzling as water drenched her from head to toe.

"Now you, princess. Off with that slicker." He started unbuttoning it and Tory tried to bat his hands away. She spat her hair out of her mouth as the wind lashed it around her, but she unbuttoned her coat one-handed, and gave it to him. Marc stuffed her water-repellent coat in with his own.

"Now your shoes." The wind and rain cut straight through Tory's thick sweater and borrowed jeans and froze her to the marrow as she struggled with the laces, eventually handing her shoes over. When he didn't respond with more than a grunt, Tory said with a giant shiver, "I don't have to tell you why I prefer hanging out with accountants. They never make me do things like this."

Marc checked over the supplies one last time. "I'll keep that in mind. Let's go."

"Go where?" She looked around for a dinghy. There was nothing in the choppy waves. Realization came too late. "Oh, no! No, I can't…"

"Hold your breath, sweet pea. Here we go." Marc took her hand and pulled her over the railing.

She'd no idea which end was up. The pressure of the black water came at her from all sides. *Don't panic, don't panic.* Water filled her nose and she panicked. Arms and legs flailing, she swallowed a mouthful of saltwater and somehow managed to bob to the surface.

She gagged, treading water as best she could. She didn't want to think of what a tasty meal her bare pink toes would make for some creature of the deep. Her right arm was useless. The most she could do was try to float it in the plastic bag. Okay, so she could swim for it—wherever "it" was.

Everything looked the same metallic gray as she scanned the water for Marc. She only had the cast on her arm to worry about. Marc was loaded down with equipment. Where was he?

A giant wave knocked her to the side, and a few seconds later she was underwater again, one-handedly trying to get the hair out of her face. It clung like seaweed. Her heart was pounding double time as she bobbed once more to the surface and then she felt something grab her sweater from behind. Tory let out a gargled scream.

"Have…a…heart…honey. If I'd wanted them to… know…we were coming I'd have sent a…telegram."

Tory was too exhausted and too relieved to see him to answer back. She relaxed marginally as he started towing her—hopefully, toward dry land. Kicking her legs and using her good arm, she tried to help. He used the swells to propel them through the surf.

Sand scored her stomach as the waves pushed them farther up the beach. For a moment she simply lay there with her face pressed to terra firma, the waves hungrily sucking at her quivering legs.

"Time to go." Marc got to his feet, pushing his dripping hair out of his face and pulling her up beside him. For one horrible moment Tory didn't think her legs would work as they reeled unsteadily. Marc's arm came out to support her, bumping her hip with whatever it was heroes wore around the waist.

The moon played hide-and-seek with the clouds, illuminating the hard planes of his face only sporadically. It started to rain. Tory sighed. "I hope we're checking into a Hilton. I'd kill for a hot bath and a cup of tea."

The rain poured down in a torrent, and she licked her lips. The water was sweet and fresh, washing away the crust of salt. Looking up to the black sky, she let the water sluice over her face and tripped over a large dead tree limb. Marc used her own momentum to keep hauling her on. She glanced around curiously. It was pretty hard to see anything in the dark. The ocean gave off a faint phosphorescence and all she could see was gray beach stretching out in front of them. Up ahead was the solid outline of a cliff.

She tugged on his hand and he stopped. Tory could just make out a feral gleam in his eyes. "I hope you don't think I'm going to climb that cliff. Because I've got to tell you—"

Afraid that he'd yell that she was slowing him down, but terrified of heights, Tory was a little relieved when she caught the faint flicker of his smile. "We're checking into the Hotel Grotta Zaffiro."

"Oh, please," Tory said fervently to his turned back, "don't be joking." He tugged her hand, leading her to the base of the cliffs. It was rockier here and her bare feet came into contact with hard stone instead of hard-packed sand.

"In twenty minutes you'll be up to your pretty neck in hot water," he promised.

Tory grinned. It sounded like heaven and gave her a new burst of energy as she scrabbled over a big boulder.

They seemed to be climbing, but it wasn't straight up. Piles of large rocks, some worn smooth by the waves, others harsh and porous, littered the base of the cliffs and they had to pick their way carefully in the dark. That hot bath was her sole focus.

Surely they would have to find a road soon? The rain

had stopped and the sky had lightened to pewter as they climbed. Marc hadn't said a word for ages. He turned to help her up.

She was out of breath and panting as she dropped her hand to her knee and hung her head, gulping for air. Her hair pooled on the rocky ground in wet, curling skeins. When she straightened, Marc was grinning.

"What?"

"You look like Medusa." He laughed softly as she gave a horrified gasp, her fingers going to her snarled and tangled hair. Taking her hand he pulled her after him. "Actually, all things considered, you look damn good. Come on, princess, your bath is waiting."

"I hope this hotel is at least a two-star— Oh, Marc, no." Disappointment rocked her back on her heels as she realized what he'd done. "Please, tell me we aren't going into a cave."

"We aren't going into a cave," he said agreeably, his fingers tightening on hers as he pulled her toward a small hole in the face of the cliff.

She saw the narrow beam of light pool at his bare feet as he turned on a flashlight, angling it so that she could find her footing behind him. It took a moment for Tory's eyes to adjust. .

"You rat, you said I'd have a hot bath." She followed behind him closely, looking anxiously about the narrow cavern. "And room service. There'd better not be any bats in here."

"No bats."

The cave smelled damp and unpleasant, but that was par for this course, Tory thought crossly. Trust him to promise a hot bath just to get her moving. They walked straight ahead for a while, then turned a corner and went straight again. They continued down a slope, walking for what felt like at least another mile.

She stumbled over a protruding rock, stubbing her toe, and then had to scurry behind him as he forged ahead. "Marc," she called, taking his hand gratefully when he stopped to wait for her.

"Okay?" His voice bounced off the narrow walls, his fingers warm as they closed more tightly over hers and he moved forward again.

"Oh, I'm just peachy." Tory lowered her voice as she heard how nervous she sounded in the echo. "Considering that the man I've trusted with my life is leading me through a cave, after lying to me about a hotel. What happens if this path runs out and there's nothing up ahead?"

"If I fall down a black hole, just let go of my hand. Someone's sure to rescue you if you go back down to the beach."

Tory's footsteps slowed at the thought that they might end up at the bottom of some deep dark hole, never to be heard from again. She shivered in her wet clothes, holding on to his hand like a lifeline. Could she let go, as he'd instructed?

Probably not, she thought, moving close enough to his back to feel the heat of his body.

The thin beam of the flashlight illuminated only a few feet in front of him. The cramped walls of the cave closed in around her, the rough surface of the rock snagging on her sweater.

After a minute or two Marc said into the silence, "I've been here before. There are no holes to fall into, I was joking. Don't worry."

Easy for him to say. Tory stuck as close as she could without tripping them both. Her bare feet hurt, as did a hundred other spots on her poor, unheroic body.

She bit her lip as they were suddenly plunged into darkness when Marc clicked off the light and stopped. "Close your eyes."

Tory was only too glad to comply. The darkness was oppressive. "Now what?"

"Trust me."

An inner voice laughed at that. "Do I have a choice?"

"No." She could hear the smile in his voice as he urged her on. "Keep 'em shut. You're going to like this."

Tory kept her eyes closed but she muttered grimly under her breath, "If it's going to be another scenario where you're the hero and I'm the shivering coward—"

"Open your eyes, princess."

Slowly Tory slitted her eyes open, then stared with eyes and mouth wide. "Marc…"

They were standing in an enormous cavern. The ceiling was a hundred feet or more above their heads. The entire area was filled with a shimmering iridescent turquoise light that made everything look somewhat unreal. In the center of the giant natural auditorium lay a placid lake. Mist floated above its surface and draped over the lush emerald ground cover and ferns at the water's edge. "Oh, Marc." She was utterly speechless. She'd never seen anything quite so beautiful in her life.

"Grotta Zaffiro," he murmured reverently. "The Sapphire Grotto."

He got just as much enjoyment from watching her expressive face as he did from the grotto and the thought of... Tory shivered and he cursed under his breath. She was exhausted, and her broken arm must hurt like hell. He'd dragged her halfway around the world and tossed her into a stormy sea. She needed food, warmth and rest.

"You can take in the sights later." Marc propelled her toward the back of the cavern. "Let's find a relatively safe place to bed down and then you can take that hot bath."

"I thought you were just joking about that too, an inducement to get me here."

Marc heard the exhausted slur of her words and kept a steadying hand on her arm. "There's a hot mineral-spring pool about three hundred yards from here." His own body felt heavy from exertion, and he was in good shape. But it had been almost three years since he'd been on an op or done anything quite this physical. For all her protestations of being a coward, she'd done amazingly well. But now her face was colorless and her lips tinged with blue.

Stopping abruptly, Marc let her sink to the sandy floor. "Rest here for a moment while I go and check out our room."

She immediately curled into a ball and closed her eyes. "'K. Call me when room service gets here...."

## CHAPTER FOUR

MARC SCOUTED the enormous cave for a safe place to bed down. Marezzo hadn't had many tourists since becoming the playground of terrorists four or five years ago. Still, he didn't want to take unnecessary risks in case some adventurous resident decided to bring guests to see the natural springs and grandeur of the grotto.

In his job, not taking the extra minute or two could be life or death—and if there was gonna be any dying, Marc thought it wasn't going to be him.

There was only one entrance—the one facing the sea in the limestone cliffs. The faint odor of sulfur assaulted his nose as he came across the small pool of steaming water. The underground spring that fed it was several hundred feet away, so the water was pleasantly hot and the smell of sulfur not too overpowering.

That hot water was going to do them both a world of good, once he'd found somewhere to stash their things.

The small space he was looking for was well hidden by a sixty-foot wall of solid limestone—a natural room of about a hundred square feet, tucked away and undetectable. Dropping his supplies on the sandy floor, he began making a rough camp. Setting up a small propane stove, he poured bottled water into a tin pot and set it to boil before going back for his reluctant partner.

She was exactly as he'd left her—curled into a small ball, wet hair trailing in the sand.

"Room service."

She was out like a light. Briefly he debated waking her so that she could take a hot bath and change into dry clothes. But she needed sleep now more than creature comforts. Picking her up, Marc made his way back to their "room." She didn't move so much as an eyelash.

Stripping naked out of his soaked clothes, Marc turned down the flame on the stove and then dried off with the clean T-shirt he retrieved from his pack.

Digging a depression in the sand, he laid down a foil survival blanket and turned to Victoria. Her mouth was slightly open. She'd be pissed if she knew she snored. Gathering her hair in both hands, he squeezed out as much saltwater as he could. Pausing with his fingers in her hair, he took stock of what the hell he was doing. Suddenly he was coldly furious with himself, realizing that somehow she'd managed to bring out a new and unfamiliar tenderness in him. In his line of work it was dangerous to be distracted.

She was trouble with a capital *T.* He didn't need to know her to realize that the very correct Miss Victoria Jones was going to be a pain in the butt. That almost kiss on Angelo's fishing tub was a surefire indication that he was slipping.

She wasn't his type. She was the kind of woman who wore her blouse buttoned to the throat, using her clothing as armor. He liked to see a woman look like a woman. Slinky clothes and FM heels. He'd always preferred women who knew the score and accepted a one-night stand. Quick, satisfying sex with no commitment. That used to be his style.

Perhaps the fact that he'd been celibate for more than three years had something to do with this newfound touchy-feely shit. Impatient with the way his thoughts were going, he pulled off her wet jeans. Her flesh was cool to the touch. And bruised. *Very* bruised.

Marc leaned back on his heels, frowning. What in the hell was this? His eyes quickly cataloged the dark splotches on her smooth skin. The marks were purple and ugly. He swore viciously under his breath. The bruising was not random. It was precise and systematic. And had probably occurred less than a month ago.

A mugging at the airport? And he'd almost believed that story? Jesus. He really *had* been away from the business for too fucking long.

Stripping off the waterlogged sweater, he checked out the rest of her body. Most of the marks were contained between her shoulders and knees. But there was no doubt that Victoria's injuries had been inflicted by a professional. A brutal expert who'd hit all the right places—ribs, kidneys, spleen—little chance of death, maximum infliction of pain. Spider?

Didn't make a whole helluva lot of sense. Spider didn't dick around. If they wanted to hurt her, she'd be dead. But if not Spider, who? He couldn't imagine this woman had many enemies. Unless it was the fashion police.

He frowned as he used a T-shirt to dry her face. The bruise on her forehead had already started to fade to a sickly yellow.

The fact that she slept through his touching her indicated just how exhausted she was. If she woke up now, she would probably bring the roof down. He trailed the warm cloth over her damp skin and couldn't tear his eyes away from her small, full, perfect breasts.

Her pale nipples peeked through the soft fabric of her bra, and he immediately decided that she was dry enough. Marc carried her to the makeshift bed several hundred yards away. She was so deeply asleep she didn't stir when he pulled a clean, dry T-shirt over her head. Covering her with another blanket, Marc first checked that the plastic had kept the cast dry and was relieved to see only a little moisture had seeped in the top. When he was sure she was as comfortable as he could make her, he grabbed a small bar of soap from the pack and went to the hot spring, where he sank up to his neck in the steaming water.

TORY AWOKE FROM A DREAM with a start, her heart pounding with terror as she sat up. But not her dream. She squeezed her eyes tightly shut. *Alex, oh, Alex, where are you? We're here. We'll find you. Just tell me where you are.*

The only sound in her head was that of her pounding heart. She tried to open her mind and concentrate, but thoughts kept crowding in and she was aware of nothing but her own fear.

Frustrated, she opened her eyes to an eerie blue glow, then inhaled the mouthwatering smell of stew. Her stomach growled. At least there was one body part that was in working order.

She felt a violent surge of panic when she realized she was alone. She glanced at the gently simmering pot at the entrance to the room. Marc couldn't have gone far if he'd left something cooking. Scrambling out of the warm cocoon of blankets, Tory realized she was wearing a knee-length black T-shirt. Her entire body blushed at the thought of Marc undressing her. Finding his backpack, she took out clean underwear and dry jeans. Normal activities took twice as long because of her sore ribs and the blasted cast.

With some contortions, she managed to pull on the jeans under the shirt. More comfortable now that she was decently covered, Tory prowled around the camp. She saw signs that Marc had dug himself in for the long haul. A large inflatable water bottle was filled and propped against the back wall next to what looked like a radio. He'd used a ledge in the rock face as a shelf for other supplies. Absently, she folded the wet clothes he'd tossed in the sand, making a mental note to rinse them somehow. The bed he'd fashioned was for two. If he'd slept there with her she didn't remember it. The last rational thought she'd had was how incredibly lovely the cavern was.

She was dying to venture out and have another good look at the beautiful expanse of freshwater, and maybe, definitely, bathe. Her hair was stiff with salt and sand.

The savory smell of the reconstituted stew drew her

to the pot. It looked as good as it smelled, activating her salivary glands and making her stomach rumble. Tory couldn't wait. For all she knew, Marc would be gone for hours. She picked up one of the forks and stabbed it into a piece of the meat.

She made herself stop eating when she realized she'd finished half the stew while crouching down beside the little propane stove. She hadn't even bothered to ladle it onto a plate. Obviously, adventure was turning her into a savage.

There wasn't much to do other than fold the top thermal blanket. After that was done, Tory laid it with perfect precision on the end of the "bed." She didn't want to think of lying there with Marc Savin for who-knew-how-many hours, wearing nothing but his shirt. She settled herself against the cool rock to wait for him. Glancing at the time, she saw without surprise that her watch had stopped. Ruined due to the long swim.

When she heard something on the other side of the rock wall she froze, then quickly scooted on her bottom into the back where the shadows were deeper.

Fool. The first thing she should have done when she woke was find some kind of weapon in that black bag of his. There was another scraping sound from the other side of the rock. Her eyes darted to the pack sitting uselessly next to the water bottle five feet away.

Someone was out there, and the smell of food would bring them right to her. Her hands started to sweat as she heard the sound of a heavy tread dragging across the sand-strewn rocks out of sight. There was a pause, then the footsteps came closer.

Tory inched against the wall toward Marc's black pack. It was probably full of all sorts of violent things. It didn't matter that she would have no idea how to use whatever she found. Hopefully, it was something big and dangerous looking. Keeping her eyes firmly fixed into the light, she reached out, her fingers touching the thin plastic skin of the pack. Holding her breath, she felt for the catch and flipped open the top. The metal ring clinked against stone. Her blood froze as the footsteps beyond her vision paused and then kept coming.

She felt something soft and pushed it impatiently aside as her hand rummaged again. Her fingers encountered something hard this time. Hard and cold and mercifully heavy.

She knew it was some sort of gun. But since she had no idea where to even begin to fire it, she figured it would make a better club. Almost suffocating on her own fear, she forced herself to take nice deep breaths as she hefted the weight in her left hand and raised it over her head.

"I hope to hell you know what to do with that thing." Marc Savin's words cut into her terror and her arm dropped. "Usually you shoot with it, but I suppose an exception can be made in your case." He looked like a modern-day pirate in his dark pants and shirt, his black hair loose and skimming his broad shoulders. He also looked annoyingly clean and alert, while she felt rumpled, out of sorts and limp as the surge of adrenaline left her system.

Tory glanced down at the nasty-looking gun still clutched in her hand. She was holding it by the barrel.

She jerked her hand away, dropping the weapon, and rose to her feet. "You scared me to death! Why didn't you call out or something?"

Marc poured what was left of the stew onto his plate. "I thought you'd still be sleeping." He sat down and dug into his meal. "Put the Uzi away and find the coffee-pot." She gaped at him and he added, "Please."

Digging out the battered pot, she filled it from the water bottle and turned up the flame on the stove. He told her where to find the coffee, then leaned his elbows on his knees.

"How are you feeling?" he asked her.

"Better than I should," Tory admitted, pouring the ground coffee into the container. When it was ready, she filled the two cups he held, then settled down to sip the hot fragrant brew. "What time is it, anyway?"

"After three. You slept for twelve hours straight."

"I wish you'd woken me." Tory clasped the warm cup between her hands, settling the container on her drawn-up knees. "I had a dream last night." Her dark hair fell over her shoulder and she set the cup down on the sand, absently fiddling with the long strand. "Alex is badly hurt, Marc. He's almost dead. I can feel it." She gazed over his shoulder without focusing, swallowing hard.

In her dream, her brother's face had been beaten so badly it was totally unrecognizable. The dream had left her shaken and frightened to death that they might be too late.

"I'll go in after dark and bring him out." His lips tightened. "I did a quick reconnoiter this morning in

Pescarna. If that's where they're holding Lynx, then they're doing a damn good job of covering their tracks. It'll save hours of time if you can pinpoint exactly where he is." Marc swallowed the last of his coffee and poured the rest of the pot into his cup. "Whatever his condition, I'll get him out. Angelo will be waiting for my signal."

She didn't like the way Marc said, "whatever his condition." Her throat was tight when she spoke. "How long do we have to wait before we can find him?"

"Can you give me his exact coordinates?"

She shook her head.

"How about a specific location?"

"Pescarna. I need to be closer…"

"No."

"You brought me all this way for exactly that purpose."

"That was before I knew they'd already gotten hold of you and beat the shit out of you."

"Oh." Did she think he couldn't figure that one out?

"Yes. *Oh.* Can you make contact with your brother and get an accurate location?"

"I'll try again." She closed her eyes, using every shred of concentration to reach out for Alex. Nothing. She tried again. And again. Finally she opened her eyes. "N-nothing. I'm sorry. He must be very weak not to pick up my call. I need to be closer."

"I hate like hell having to take you at all. Once you locate him, I'll bring you back here. We have a few hours to kill until dark." He tossed her a towel and a small bar of soap. "If you turn left and go about a hundred feet you'll find your hot bath. Take your time."

He pulled her to her feet. "I'll be at the main entrance, keeping a lookout."

Tory set her cup next to his on a rock ledge. "To tell the truth, I'd be more excited if you told me there was a bathroom around here." Flushing, she picked up the wet, folded clothes, adding them to the soap and towel.

"Your every wish is my command. Follow me."

The cavern was about the size of two football fields, the walls pale in the eerie glow. The sapphire water was crystal clear, casting shimmering waves on the walls.

Tory walked beside Marc as they circled the lake on the far side. "How do all these plants live in here?" she asked as they passed a shrub covered with tiny white flowers. Ferns and moss grew right to the water's edge.

"There's plenty of natural light and freshwater." Marc plucked one of the flowers and stuck it in her braid. "Let me know if you want to swim, though. The water here is over forty-five feet deep. Its clarity is deceptive."

Circling around a huge fern that was as tall as he was, he turned back to look at her. "See that whirlpool at the end?"

In this light, with the reflection from the lake, his eyes were crystal clear and looked blue. "What is it?"

"A natural drain." He pointed back the way they'd come. "The hot spring is back there in the gut of the mountain. The water pools in the depression near camp and then runs into this lake. By then it's cold. The water drains down a forty-foot tunnel directly into the sea below. Don't swim here unless I'm with you. That drain hole is wide enough to suck you right down to the rocks below." Tory shivered. She'd had enough of deep water yesterday when he'd dragged her overboard.

He pointed out the cement enclosed bathroom standing sentinel discreetly around the corner from the entrance. "Only the one on the left still works. They were stuck in here for the tourists, but there haven't been any visitors to the grotto in years."

"Why not? The cavern is the most beautiful thing I've ever seen."

"Remember the rocks we climbed to get here yesterday? Those crashed down from the cliffs. It isn't safe for tourists at the moment. Besides, since the terrorists claimed Marezzo, they've discouraged tourism to a certain extent. A few tour groups are allowed in every now and then to preserve their cover. But it's pretty much their island. The locals are all basically keeping a conspiracy of silence. Their lives depend on it."

Marc pulled the Walther from the small of his back and checked it, ignoring the way Victoria's eyes widened at the sight of the weapon. "I'll be just outside if you need me. The hot spring is back the way we came."

THE POOL WAS ABOUT six feet across and surrounded by water-smoothed rock. The bottom was a powdery sand. Tory stripped quickly, then stepped into the hot water, keeping her arm out and dry. The heat felt wonderful as she sank in up to her chin, her hair floating around her. Sighing deeply as her aching muscles relaxed in the warmth, she closed her eyes against the steam.

It felt like minutes, but was probably more like half

an hour when the sound of his footsteps was followed by his irritated voice. "What in the hell do you think you're doing?"

Tory shrieked as she blinked her eyes open to see Marc Savin emerge through the steam. Water splashed over the side of the pool as she slithered upright, her hand to her throat.

"What are you doing here?" she gasped. She'd fallen asleep and it took a moment for her brain to kick into gear. Her cheeks flamed as his cold gaze drifted down to where her wet hair clung to her bare skin.

"What's taking you so long?"

One arm was useless as a cover. Tory quickly whipped the towel off the rocks and into the water and slapped it over her chest; her knees made little islands above the water as she drew them up to cover as much of herself as she could. "I must have fallen asleep. Look, I'll just finish up here and… Would you please leave?" Mortification made her voice choke. She flushed from her hair to her toes.

He came closer. Tory licked her lips and slid farther under the water with a one-handed death grip on the towel. "Please. Just go." She was afraid to blink. He was already far too close.

He was wearing jeans. *Just* jeans. His naked chest was darkly tanned, a thick trail of crisp black hair ran in a V down the center. He crouched beside the pool, his knees spread for balance. Flushing even more, Tory ripped her gaze away from what was now at eye level. If she'd reached out her hand she could have touched him, he was that close.

Her heart rose to her throat. She didn't know where to look. Tory stifled a whimper.

Steam moved in lazy swirls around him. His hair was still loose, hanging to his shoulders in a dark shiny drift that was disconcerting. She stared at a distant point on the other side of the cave. The wet terry across her chest felt heavy, forcing her to take deeper breaths. She could feel his stare like fingers sliding down her naked skin, and she shivered.

Managing to look him in the eye she again said in a small voice, "Please. Will you just go away?"

Marc stared down at the woman in the water. The steam shimmered on her pink skin. It looked smooth and soft. Her wet hair effectively blanketed her body, trailing in the water like seaweed. A fragrant blob of soapsuds slid down her silky shoulder, and dropped to float on top of the water. He knew he should leave. It was absolutely crazy to have come looking for her in the first place.

Even the center part in her hair was pink with embarrassment.

"We'll be leaving as soon as it's dark," he said briskly, shifting to his feet. Her face went even redder as he turned back to look at her.

"Fine," she managed, eyeing him warily. He could see the frantic pulse in her throat. Christ. He was going to have a hell of a time with her. She was such a little mouse. She quivered if he even looked at her.

"I'll get you a dry towel." He glanced at the wet material molded to her breasts as she shifted restlessly.

"Thank you," she said stiffly.

Perversely, Marc stayed. He couldn't afford to have her fold like a wet tissue when they found her brother. He couldn't afford for her to get all weepy and terrified every time he snapped out an order. An order that could very well mean life or death. He needed her tough. He needed her mad. He needed her to grow a spine. Fast.

Tory hating him for being a sadistic bully might just be a perk, he thought wryly, watching the heat spread across her cheeks. Since he was having a hard time keeping his hands off her, it worked to his advantage if she loathed him. Yeah. This might work out just fine.

"You sound like a prim little schoolgirl," he said mockingly. "Can't you say anything other than 'Thank you'?"

Her head tilted regally. "Yes. I can say go away!"

"Princess, there's nothing here that would make me want to stay." The way she tilted that chin irritated the hell out of him. He wanted to see just how far he would have to push her for her to fight back. He sighed. It was a useless endeavor. She hadn't been kidding when she'd said she was a coward.

"I hate you," she said in her quiet little voice, looking at anything but him.

"Say it louder."

Her eyes shot back to his face. "Wh-what?"

"Say it louder and with feeling. Let me see how much you hate me."

"You're crazy."

Marc took the three steps required to reach her side again. He crouched down and took her chin in his hand. Her eyes were wide and frightened. "Let me see some grit and backbone, lady. I'm already having second thoughts about hauling your ass to Marezzo."

"I *told* you I didn't want to come."

"Yeah, you did," he said roughly. He dropped his hand from the damp heat of her face and levered himself to his feet. "I'd feel a little more confident if you showed some guts. Hell, I'd settle for spunk."

"You want spunk?" Her eyes blazed. "How's this for spunk?" Whipping the soaking towel off her chest, she threw it at him with all her strength.

The soaking fabric flopped down harmlessly into the sand. Marc kept his gaze on her face with effort. Her eyes shot emerald sparks at him, and her jaw was rigid. "I'm here on Marezzo with you. I'm here, but I don't like it." Her voice rose. "And I certainly don't like you." She threw the soap next; it glanced off a button on his fly and dropped behind a fern.

"I'll give you spunk!" She picked up a small smooth stone, throwing that, too.

Marc grinned as it missed his head by two feet. "Atta girl."

"You're a loathsome man."

"Yeah?" Marc smiled. There was hope for her yet.

"Yes! Stop taunting me…and go…away!"

"Or what?"

Victoria looked at him. He was cocky and arrogant and just too blasted sure of himself. She'd read about men like this. She might need him to find Alex, but that didn't mean that she had to like him. She stared at his insolent face. She needed to establish right now that she wasn't just going to take everything he dished out. But how?

He loomed over her, bare feet spread, arms folded over his naked chest. He knew that she was rattled and he was having a fine old time at her expense. What could she do that would rattle *his* cage?

Before she could really think the action all the way through, Tory rose from the water. Keeping her gaze fixed at a point to the left and behind Marc, she stepped onto the rocks on the rim and then moved around him. Water sluiced down the goose bumps on her skin. Every nerve and cell in her body was embarrassed, but she kept her back straight and her head high as she walked past him covered in nothing but her long hair and what was left of her dignity. Her face burned, but not for anything in the world would she let him see how shaken she was and how much courage it had taken for her to get out of that pool naked.

She felt totally exposed and more vulnerable than she'd ever felt before. But she wouldn't back down. Mingled with her embarrassment was the sudden realization of the guts it had taken.

Oh, my God, she thought incredulously as she heard his startled gasp behind her. I did it! Her spine rigid, Tory forced her footsteps to stay even and refused to give in to the temptation to run and cover herself. There was no sound from behind her, but she would have been hard-pressed to hear anything over the thundering of her heart. She was five steps from the entrance to the camp when a hand gripped her upper arm. She bit back a scream. Marc swung her around to face him. There was a nasty glitter in his pale eyes. "Sex doesn't mean a damn thing to me. Got that? So don't throw that delectable little body in front of me anymore, because I'm just not buying."

Without a blink, Tory stood frozen in his grasp. His lips were a hard thin line and his eyes were narrowed on her face. Inwardly she flinched at the iciness of his expression. Her heart was beating hard enough to make her body shudder.

What a nasty excuse for a human being he was. "How dare you! I wasn't throw—" She'd been trying to prove a point, but in doing so she'd left her actions up for interpretation. And Marc Savin being Marc Savin had taken it as sexual instead of as a show of…independence? No, Tory thought with a lump in her throat. *Stupidity.* She dropped her eyes, fighting back tears of embarrassment. After a few moments she forced herself to look up at him.

His face was as inscrutable as the Sphinx. She swallowed. "I wasn't trying to… I didn't mean… I… I don't like being bullied."

"I told you I wanted to see a little backbone. I didn't mean I wanted to see you buck naked."

She was gritting her teeth so hard her jaw ached. "I'm going to get dressed now."

"Do that."

Marc gave her a good fifteen minutes to get her emotional shit together. Hell, to be honest with himself, he needed a minute to get his own shit together. Lord. What a body. She was luscious from head to toe. And it wasn't bruises he'd been looking at this time.

Victoria Jones was the sister of his best friend, Marc reminded himself. Off-limits. Out-of-bounds. Besides, she wasn't his type.

Yeah? he mocked, all that silky long hair? The firm, creamy skin? Those long legs? Those beautiful, pink-tipped full breasts? The mouth that would tempt a saint? Right. Not his type at all.

When he went back into their small camp she was sitting in the middle of the makeshift bed, cradling her arm, wet hair soaking the shirt she'd pulled on over her damp naked body. She wasn't giving an inch. From the little he knew of her, he was astounded that she'd dredged up the nerve to pull that stunt. His eyes narrowed in speculation.

He'd known before they started out that she'd be a pain in the ass. But damn it, he needed her to find her brother. He didn't have a choice. On the other hand, he mused with great annoyance, he hadn't given her any choice, either. The coffee in the metal cup was cold. Marc drank it anyway, irritated as she gave a little sniff. Good. Back to her usual modus operandi. Marc didn't acknowledge the relief he felt. Victoria Jones, the wimp, he could handle.

He crouched down beside her. His soap smelled completely different on her skin. "What happened? Does something hurt?" When she didn't respond, he lifted her chin to look into her face. "Are you sick? Does your arm hurt? Are you embarrassed that I saw you naked? What?" Her eyes filled with tears. Great. "Talk to me." His voice came out a little harsher than it should have.

"Leave me alone." She glared at him, the tears making her green eyes glitter. "I broke the comb. Okay? I broke the blasted comb!"

Marc stared at her as if she'd lost her mind. "You're crying because you broke a damn comb? Christ, lady, it's a fine day when that's the worst thing that happens to you."

He got to his feet impatiently, paced to the back of the cave and pulled out the sat phone. If she was going to freak out over something as ridiculous as a broken comb, they were in big trouble.

He'd been delusional to think he could get her to grow some kind of backbone. He couldn't make her something that she wasn't. Not her fault, damn it.

Pushing her hair aside she looked over her shoulder. "What are…are you doing?"

"Calling Angelo. He can come and get you."

## CHAPTER FIVE

MARC WAITED for Angelo to pick up the phone. Damn fool woman. He'd schlepped her halfway around the world because he needed her to find Alex. Fast. Faster than he could do it himself. But she was proving to be more of a liability than an asset.

"No!" Tory jumped up, tears forgotten. "No, d-don't do that." She grabbed the phone and disconnected. "I'm the only one who can find my brother. You said so."

"Lady, I must have been out of my ever-loving mind to think you'd be any help." He took the phone from her, deliberated for a second, then stuck it in his back pocket. "Look at you. You're already falling apart and we haven't even gotten to the hard part yet."

"You don't understand." She bit her lip. "It's not...I can't get the knots out of my hair. The comb broke, and I... The comb's broken."

He'd known her for little more than a day and in that short time he had her figured. She was a lousy liar, which he liked. She was too damned sexy without being aware of it, which he didn't like. Marc remembered the prissy, navy suit and sensible heels she'd worn when he'd first met her. He had a sudden mental image of her straightening her collar and striving to neaten her hair when she'd awakened in his den the other night.

He might not know her well, but one thing he did know was that she was obsessive about being neat and right now her bare feet were sandy, the T-shirt she wore was crumpled from being in the pack, and her hair was wildly tangled. She was a mess.

He liked her this way. Rumpled and untidy. But clearly it wasn't a look she was comfortable with.

"Come here," he said gently. With a hand on her shoulder, he pushed her down on the blanket and settled behind her. "Give me the comb."

Her slender shoulders were rigid under his hands. "I don't want you to touch me, thank you very much."

"I don't want to be kept up all damn night because you're sniveling about your frigging hair. Give me the comb."

She handed the largest piece of the broken comb to him over her shoulder.

"Relax." He picked up the towel and rubbed at her hair.

Her voice sounded muffled and sheepish. "My mother used to do this."

He rubbed out as much of the moisture as he could, then picked up the comb. Her hair pooled on the silver blanket between them, and he picked up the ends and started drawing the teeth through the wet tangles.

"Tell me about her," he said softly. Her hair felt like silk in his fingers.

"I don't have that many memories. I do remember that she and my father were inseparable." Her voice caught and she cleared her throat before continuing.

"My father was a stuntman, and my mother always went with him on shoots. Apparently he was in high demand, because they were gone a lot."

"And where were you when they were 'gone a lot'?"

"I lived with Grandmother most of the time."

*And were brainwashed by her, too,* Marc thought, angry on her behalf. "And where did your brother live?"

"Boarding school…for a while. When we were eight they didn't come back."

Marc smoothed her hair across his knee. "What happened?"

"They were killed while Dad was filming in Spain. The small commuter plane crashed on the way to the shoot. My grandmother kept me. She sent Alex to foster care." Her shoulders hitched. "We hated being separated like that."

"What the hell?" What kind of person separated siblings, especially twins?

"He went from home to home. He couldn't be adopted— Grandmother wouldn't allow it. She adopted me. But she wouldn't adopt Alex."

"Why not?"

"Because of her age the State wouldn't allow her to keep both of us. At least that's what she claimed. That was probably partially the reason, but I think it was also because she felt a little guilty not taking him, and wanted to keep that tenuous connection."

*What a bitch.* "And by doing so prevented him from having any home at all."

"Yes," Tory bowed her head as he continued combing. "She disliked men in general. She'd had an abusive childhood and hated her own father. She got married because in those days it was the only thing for a woman to do, but the marriage was short-lived. Her husband passed away before my mother was born."

Grandmother sounded like a piece of work. No wonder Tory was so repressed. It also went a long way in explaining her old-fashioned clothing and attitude, and the strong attachment to her wandering brother. "Did she kill him?" Marc asked drily.

"I don't think so, although I think she was certainly capable of doing so."

Marc bet there were any number of skeletons in Granny's closet. "So why do you have different last names?"

"She'd reverted back to her maiden name after her husband died. It was easier for us to have the same name."

It also explained how Lynx had managed to keep a twin sister under wraps. Marc felt a swell of compassion for her, which annoyed the hell out of him. He frowned. He didn't have time for that kind of emotion on a mission. His senses had to be razor sharp or they were all going to end up dead.

"We could communicate telepathically, but we didn't see each other again for almost eight years. I hated it," she said fiercely.

Marc felt the tension in her back. He kept combing.

"I did everything right so that she would bring Alex home. She wanted a nice, quiet, neat little girl. And that's what I was. She was my only security, and I had to do everything perfectly so she wouldn't s-send me away, too." Marc heard the tears in her voice. He could imagine her as a small child. Neat, quiet and waiting for her brother to come home. No wonder she was so fanatically neat and tidy. No wonder she didn't like her quiet little world turned upside down. She'd had enough of that as a child.

Her hair was tangle free and almost dry, but Marc kept running the broken comb through it. "When we were eighteen, Alex disappeared."

Marc knew where he'd gone. He'd recruited Alex Stone right off the street when the boy had been well on his way to becoming an accomplished car thief.

"My grandmother got sick. I nursed her till she died. Then I took the money she left me and bought a condo—" her voice hardened "—with two bedrooms. And I made a home for us…Alex and me." She twisted to look at him. "That was my revenge. I could make a home for us using her money."

But it had been too late for Alex Stone, Marc thought grimly. By then he was "Lynx." And that had left his sister out—again. He forced himself to section off three heavy ropes of her hair. She handed him the tie over her shoulder when he'd finished the braid. "Thank you." She asked quietly, "You are going to find Alexander, aren't you, Marc?" Her hair had soaked her T-shirt. The thin wet cotton lovingly accented the sweet full curves of her breasts.

"Don't worry, I'll find him. By this time tomorrow the two of you will be living it up in Rome."

Her eyes glowed. "Really?"

He'd felt the first unwelcome stirring of desire for

her on the boat. No big deal. He hadn't acted on it. He'd seen her naked. Again, no big deal. He'd certainly seen more than his fair share of naked women. "Yeah." At first he'd dismissed the attraction, thinking it was because of her hair. He'd never had a thing about a woman's hair before. But images of being tangled in yards of Tory's dark silky hair had him hot and bothered. He'd almost managed to convince himself, while soaking in the hot spring, that he was in full control of his body's urges.

He'd been dead wrong.

"Thank you." Her lips were pale, her teeth very white as she gave him a shy smile.

Using both thumbs, Marc brushed away the tears drying on her cheeks, then cupped her face. He shouldn't do this, he knew. The op had barely begun. He kissed her damp eyelids, and she made a murmuring protest as his fingers tangled in her hair, pushing gently so that she fell backward, half on the blanket and half on the sand.

He just wanted a small taste of her, that was all. One small taste. He settled his mouth over hers. She tasted of toothpaste, minty and fresh. He slanted his mouth and her lips opened under his. Just a little. Just enough so he could slide his tongue between her teeth. God, it was sweet heaven.

It shouldn't have been this good. As she tentatively, shyly, touched her tongue to his, Marc thought he would jump out of his skin. He forced his hands to stay in her hair. He wanted to strip her naked and drive into her with a force that rocked him. Tearing his mouth away from hers, he sat up, running his fingers around the back of his neck until he could control his ragged breathing. She lay there watching him with those big slumberous green eyes, her lips wet and swollen from his kiss, her breathing as unsteady as his own.

"This was one bad idea, princess. Roll over and get a little more shut-eye before we go."

TORY WOKE TO DARKNESS and the single glow of the propane stove. Marc was a shadow in the shadows in his dark clothes, his expression closed. "You have time to eat before we go."

Tory self-consciously ran her hand over her eyes. "I'm not hungry."

"You need to eat anyway." He rose and dished up her meal, bringing it over to her. Tory pulled the thin blanket to her chest. She wished with all her heart that she was wearing a bra.

"Honey, I've already seen everything you've got. It'll take us at least forty minutes to get to Pescarna and it's after eleven now." He pushed a fork into her hand, his eyes deliberately cold. "I hope to God you aren't expecting a big declaration. It was only a kiss. I don't plan on analyzing every damned body function between now and when we leave."

She looked up at him. "Thanks for putting that into perspective." She cocked her head and her braid slithered over one shoulder. "If I'd known I'd be reduced to a 'body function' I wouldn't have bothered kissing you back," she snapped. Setting the full plate aside, she tossed off the blanket and rose. His jaw tightened as he gritted his teeth. She must have caught the feral gleam in his eyes for she said sweetly, "All you had to do was say no."

"Hell, you didn't even know what you were offering."

Victoria tilted her chin at him. "I don't remember my offering you anything."

"How's it feel to be the last American virgin, honey?" Marc asked sarcastically, wanting her to get angry and slug him, in which case he'd grab her and— *You've lost your mind, Phantom. Get a grip on your damned hormones. This is like a jackal taunting a kitten.*

Her nose turned pink. "It feels quite comfortable, thank you."

Marc took the sucker punch like a man. He'd been joking! "I thought the definition of a virgin was an ugly thirteen-year-old."

Victoria gave him a dirty look. "I was an ugly thirteen-year-old. I'm also a realistic twenty-six-year-old. I like my life just the way it is, thank you very much. I didn't ask you to maul me, and I don't appreciate being taunted just because I have principles. My virginity is my business, and I'll thank you to keep your sweaty hands off me."

"Princess, sex is a sweaty business. I bet if you loosened up a little it would grow on you. Close your eyes and imagine two sweaty bodies rubbing against each other…."

"Why do you insist on talking to me like this?" Tory's eyes flashed. "I know you don't like me. Fine, the feeling is absolutely mutual. You were the one who dragged me here, remember?"

"Wow. You're really scaring me to death," he said mockingly, stalking her across the sand.

Tory stood her ground as he came toward her. She pulled the Uzi out of his pack—right side up this time. It looked ridiculous in her small hands.

He stepped right up to her so that the cool metal poked him in the chest. "Don't ever point a weapon at a person unless you mean it," he rasped. His hand shot out and gripped her wrist like a vise.

She tried to jerk her arm away. "Oh, I mean it."

Marc took the Uzi away from her and set it on top of the pack. Her face looked pale and vulnerable in the dim light as she moved away from him. "We're going to have to cover that cast. People will be able to see it a mile away. Here." He tossed her a long-sleeved black sweatshirt.

A virgin. At twenty-six? In this day and age? Christ, that was one for the Guinness book. Marc tossed her a pair of black running shoes.

"Make sure none of that white shows." He pointed, and she pulled the sleeve down over her cast. He'd borrowed the clothes and shoes from the son of one of his ranch hands. They looked a hell of a lot different on Tory than they had on the kid. He handed her a stick of black camo paint. "Use this on the part that shows… Yeah, right there between your fingers. Sure you can handle this?"

She didn't misinterpret the question. She handed back the paint stick. "I'll do whatever it takes to get Alex back," she said grimly, tucking her hair down the back of the sweatshirt. "*Whatever* it takes."

A FULL MOON LIT THEIR WAY down the rocks to the beach. Because it was high tide they kept close to the base of the rocky cliffs. The full moon painted ribbons of silver on the dark water and reflected off the sand. The scene was like a dramatic black-and-white photograph.

The night was quiet except for the crashing of waves against the rocks and the hissing as water washed up in foamy patterns on the wet sand.

"When we get into Pescarna," Marc said quietly, "locate your brother and I'll bring you back to camp. I'll do the rest." He took her hand to help her over the slippery boulders.

Tory grunted. It was harder going than she'd imagined. Marc was like a cat as he jumped from one huge rock to another. She knew that she was slowing him down. But she was scared of slipping into the wildly foaming surf churning among the rocks. The clean, fresh scent of the sea was heady in the warm still air as she stumbled after him.

He'd told her that Pescarna was only four miles up the coast. It felt a lot farther. She almost ran into Marc's back because she wasn't concentrating. "What?"

He put his hand over her mouth. "Shh," he whispered. "We're here." His eyes glittered in the moonlight. "Turn on your…brother radar so we know which way to go."

Tory closed her eyes and forced her mind to clear. *Alex?*

She could hear the pounding of the waves behind them and in the distance the faint sound of someone singing. Every now and then a fine mist of ocean spray reached them, beading on their clothes.

*Alex?* Alex. Alex. Alex.

"Hey." She felt Marc's arm come around her. "Hey!" He pulled her into the circle of his strong arms and pressed her face to his damp sweater. He smelled like the sea. "Relax, you're hyperventilating."

"Oh, God, Marc. I can't sense his presence at all."

The pressure of his hand rubbing up and down her back was strangely comforting. "Just relax, honey, and open your mind. If Lynx is around he'll know we're here. I thought you said you could tune him in at will? Just close your eyes and concentrate."

Try as she might, Tory didn't get any response to her desperate mental pleas. She shuddered, her arms tightening around Marc's waist. "There's nothing," she said in a small voice. "Nothing." She looked up into his face. "Maybe I need to be closer. If Alex is badly hurt he might not be able to communicate from this distance."

"Damn. How close?"

*Very.* "I won't know until I find him."

Marc brushed the bangs out of her eyes. "Just don't do anything st—rash."

Tory smiled. "I'm a coward, remember?"

"Yeah. I remember." Marc took her hand and drew her over the next series of rocks. "Closer it is. Do everything I tell you, and stick to me like glue for the duration. Got it?"

She wouldn't want it any other way. "Got it."

Sand gave way to scrub grass and the lights of

Pescarna twinkled against the night sky. Then she felt the reassuring solidity of cobblestones under her feet. She followed Marc into the shadow of an overhanging wrought-iron balcony. The spicy smell of geraniums permeated the air. The street was narrow and the cobblestones bit into the soles of her shoes as Tory clutched Marc's hand and continued on behind him, straining to hear him as he murmured, "We're going to just keep moving until you get something."

Soon whitewashed Moorish-style houses rose like cliffs on either side of them. There were no people in the streets this late at night, but they could hear loud voices coming through the open windows. A canary chirped, and dishes rattled.

Blood-red geraniums spilled over balconies, and the aroma of garlic and tomato filled the warm night. The sweatshirt was too hot, but it covered the white of her cast. She concentrated all her thoughts on Alex.

An hour passed and then another. They slipped up one narrow alleyway and down the next, pausing often for Tory to concentrate. Nothing. She wanted to cry, but one look at Marc's stony expression froze the tears.

The fishing village was small, but by the time they had traversed every street and alley twice, Tory was beyond tears. They emerged on the far side of the village and stood hidden in the shadow of a small grove of olive trees.

Clouds whispered across the moon. Everything was still. A dog barked, then it, too, fell silent. Tory rested her head against the gnarled trunk of a tree. "I'm sorry."

Marc longed to comfort her, but he, too, was frustrated. "We'll go back to camp and I'll have Angelo come and get you." He put a heavy arm around her slumped shoulders. "Come on. I think you've had enough for one night."

They circled the village, keeping to the shadows on the beach. The smell of fish was overpowering as they passed the dark silhouettes of the fishing boats.

Suddenly Tory grabbed his arm and pulled him into a doorway. The windows were dark in the narrow three-story house, Everything was quiet.

"Alex was here!" she whispered, heart pounding. "But... Oh, God, Marc. They've taken him some-where else."

She shivered, her hand clutching his tightly. "They took him away within the last six or eight hours. No more."

"How do you know how long— Never mind. Time for you to go home, princess." The words were merely a breath in the still, fragrant night air.

*"No,"* Tory whispered, just as quietly. "Not until we find him."

A window down the street slid open and a man stuck out his head. *"Zitto! Se ne vada!"*

Heart in her throat, she froze. "Was that...?" *One of the bad guys?*

Marc shook his head. "Local. He wants us to get the hell out of Dodge. Let's go."

They kept deep in shadow until they reached the end of the street. Tory stopped and tugged on his hand. "There's a back way, down this alley. Come on."

She saw Marc's eyes light up suspiciously. "How do you know there's a back way?"

She stepped over a pile of refuse from the trattoria, still dragging him along. "You don't want to know."

They stopped under a small cement balcony. Marc grabbed her shoulder and spun her around. "I sure as hell *do* want to know. Look at me." He held her chin. "There's something stinking in Denmark and I want to know what it is."

"It's that pile of— Ow!"

"Start talking, and make it quick." A muscle twitched in his cheek as he pinned her in place.

"I—I had the dubious pleasure of being a guest here for a—for a while."

Christ. He'd been away from the business for too goddamned long when the fact that a woman showing up on his doorstep, bruised, battered and broken, having been in Marezzo, didn't warrant immediate explanation. Marc hadn't realized just how fucking apathetic he'd become. "When?" he demanded, knowing he was a day late and a dollar short on the questioning.

"Just before I went to Brandon to find you.

"And you're only mentioning this *now?*" He spoke in his normal tone—furious. He practically dragged her down the alley and didn't stop until they were back in the small olive grove.

"Start at the beginning and keep going."

"I told you I came to look for Alex."

Her troubled eyes met his and Marc forced himself to remain calm. He kept enough distance between them so that he wasn't tempted to strangle her. Although to be fair, if he'd asked her the right questions the other day, he wouldn't be having to ask them now. Three years of shoveling horse shit had made him forget the important shit *people* hid. It was his job, *his* job, damn it, to know things before they reared up and bit him in the ass.

"I spent a week playing tourist in *Pavina*. Alex wasn't there. I rented a Vespa and came to this side of the island. I knew he was close, so I checked into a *pensione*." She shivered, although the sweatshirt was clinging uncomfortably to her sweaty back. "I guess I…I guess I asked one too many questions."

"Shit, Victoria!"

"Stop cursing me."

"Get on with the story."

"Two men came and told me that they had some questions. They weren't very polite about it, and they scared me to death. I tried to blow them off by telling them I was on vacation but they got…nasty."

Marc growled low in his throat like a rabid dog. Damn fool woman. "What did they do to you?"

"They took me to that pink house and asked me what I was doing here poking around. I kept lying to them. They didn't take it well. I wished I spoke fluent Italian, but I just caught a few words here and there. They were yelling and screaming and waving their hands."

"Cut to the chase."

"Yes, well, that went on for a while, and then they locked me in a room upstairs and they told me to think about it. Which I did." Victoria's eyes went unfocused. "They came back and I stuck to my story and the big one in the expensive suit hit me…and the other one got mad and hit him. And they were yelling and screaming again. And then a man came and they…they tied me…. And then I started screaming…." She picked an olive off the ground, grimacing when she bit into it. She spat it neatly in her hand, then buried the soggy pieces in a hole she made in the dirt.

His jaw ached from clenching his teeth. "How long did they hold you?"

"Thirteen days, seven hours and eighteen minutes."

"How did you get out?"

"I convinced them I was telling the truth. Besides, they knew that I had to see a doctor about my arm. That's what they said. It didn't ring true but I didn't care, I was just grateful to be out of there. They took me to the airport and sent me to Naples."

It didn't make sense. Why would they keep her for almost two weeks and then let her go? "Stay here. I'm going back to check it out. Don't move, Victoria. You understand me? Don't budge an inch. If you see anyone coming, move slowly back into the cover of the trees. If I'm not back in an hour, go to camp."

Tory watched him until he blended into the shadows at the edge of the village and faded from sight. Please God, let him come back within the hour. She had no intention of finding her way across the rocks alone. She swallowed as she remembered those days and nights in that house.

The last thing she'd imagined was that he would haul her all over God's creation and bring her back here. But it was worth it—anything was worth it if she could find Alex.

They had done a little more than "hit" her. By the
time she arrived in Naples, she was so weak from lack
of food and the beatings that she'd collapsed at the
airport. She'd been taken to the hospital. There she'd
been treated with what she thought was a pretty cavalier
attitude. The authorities believed that her husband had
beaten her, and Tory was too scared to tell them the
truth. She didn't want to risk making matters worse for
Alex.

She rested her head against the olive tree and kept
her eyes firmly fixed on the spot where Marc had disappeared. She didn't want to remember her ordeal. The
pain had been excruciating. The terror had been worse.
It had surpassed her worst nightmare, because never in
her wildest imagination had she conceived of a human
being doing what they had done to her.

What had made it a million times worse was that
she'd felt Alex close by. Alex had known exactly what
they were doing to her and had been powerless to stop
them. Tears welled in her eyes and she gritted her teeth.

She would do anything to get her brother away from
them. Tory pressed the heel of her hand against her
eyes, willing the useless tears away.

"Alex, where *are* you?"

# CHAPTER SIX

"DID YOU FIND ANYTHING?" she asked eagerly, standing and dusting the dirt off her backside when Marc returned almost an hour later.

"They have him in *Pavina*."

"Good." She took an eager step forward. "Let's go."

He shook his head. "It's going to be light in a couple of hours. I'll wait to go in." There'd been three men in the house. Marc had eavesdropped long enough to get a general location on Lynx. And the fact that he, or rather *someone* from T-FLAC, was expected and eagerly anticipated. Since he had no garbage detail for backup, he'd left them alive. Dead bodies had a tendency to set off alarms.

After a moment's hesitation, she nodded and they silently skirted town before heading to the beach. It was worse going back. Thick clouds had covered the moon, making it impossible for her to see one foot in front of the other. Marc, on the other hand, seemed to have perfect vision as he pushed her up one side of an enormous boulder, then practically dragged her down the next. By the time they got to the grotto, her legs were shaky and her breathing erratic. She wasn't used to such strenuous exercise. Marc hadn't slowed down just because she was out of shape.

Pulling the Walther from his belt, he checked it before he laid it next to the pallet. "We'll go into *Pavina* tomorrow." He pulled his black T-shirt over his head.

Tory couldn't tear her eyes away from sleek muscles and taut, tanned skin. An arrow of crisp, curling dark hair ran down his washboard-flat stomach to the waist-band of his jeans. He started unzipping his fly, and Tory swallowed audibly as a vee of paler skin was exposed. And then Marc, wearing nothing but skimpy black briefs, settled himself comfortably on top of the silver thermal blanket.

"Best get some sleep, princess. Tomorrow's going to be a long day." He pillowed his arms beneath his head, his eyes narrowed as he watched her. Tory picked up his discarded jeans, folded them, then placed them by the water bottle and picked up his shirt. It smelled like him, hot and sexy. She forced herself to fold it neatly on top of the jeans.

"I slept all day. I'm not tired." There was nothing else to tidy. While the idea of leaving her brother wherever he was made Tory's heart falter, she had to trust that Marc knew what he was doing. But waiting until dark to go looking again meant an entire day trapped in the cave with Marc. Her grandmother would have said she had ants in her pants. She would have been partially right.

It annoyed her that he looked so relaxed while she was as wound up as an old-fashioned watch spring. She wished that he'd left his jeans on. Unwillingly, her eyes traveled down the long length of his practically naked body.

"Come over here, then," he said, his voice silky soft in the half-light. "I'll show you what we can do instead of sleeping." Tory grabbed the bar of soap out of the pack and picked up a damp towel. "I'm going to take a bath."

Marc closed his eyes, a small smile playing around his mouth. "Don't wake me when you come to bed."

He made it sound so…intimate. She scowled as she walked out of camp. As soon as she saw the hot steaming water in the small circular pool she started pulling the damp sweatshirt over her head. The jeans came next. It was a good thing she could use her arm a little now.

Sliding slowly into the water, she rested the cast on the ledge of rock and closed her eyes as the hot water soothed her aching muscles. The water was relaxing. She started soaping herself before zoning out in the soporific heat of the water. Her skin jumped as her soapy hand skimmed her body. What would it be like…? She pushed that thought out of her mind. Marc Savin was dangerous; he made her think of things she'd never imagined. He made her want things that she'd only read about. How could just spending a few days with the man turn her thoughts from rational to irrational?

The thought of his hand on her breast made her skin shiver. Oh, God. All she could think about when he was anywhere near her was his touch on her bare skin. The way his hands had felt caressing her hair. Somehow the combination of danger and the proximity of Marc were enough to make her crazy. Only a crazy woman would be fantasizing about a man who couldn't be more wrong, more ill-suited for the life she'd chosen for herself. She wanted nesting and consistency. Home and family—things a man like Marc probably mocked in his sleep. Correction—he probably mocked them openly— Lord knew he wasn't one to keep his opinion to himself.

So, it had to be a situational psychotic break. There was something compellingly erotic about the danger mixed with an unhealthy dose of pent-up sexual frustration on her part.

She played the What If game in her mind. She'd never fit into his life. He liked danger. She'd seen the anticipation on his face as they'd surveyed the sleeping town of Pescarna.

She just wanted to find Alex and go back to her quiet, predictable, normal life. She wanted to go back to her color-coordinated wardrobe—so what if it was all neutrals? She wanted her safe, comfortable eight-to-five job at the auto-parts store.

She didn't like adventure. It was fine to read about it, but she was already good and sick of living it. And Marc Savin scared her, most of all. It wasn't just the fact that he held a gun like a natural extension of his arm. When he'd kissed her she'd forgotten every single thing her grandmother had ever warned her about. And there had been a ton of overprotective warnings delivered over the years.

Shivering despite the hot water, she laid the tie from the end of her braid carefully on her folded clothes and let her hair fan around her. She wanted shampoo and conditioner—not utilitarian soap. Soap she shared with Marc. Impatiently she lathered her hair and sank beneath the surface to rinse it.

Marc wasn't for her. They were as different as chalk from cheese. When she got back to her real world she would forget all about him and get on with her life. The only reason her mind was consumed with him at all was because of the close proximity. It wasn't as if he could go unnoticed. He was large, menacing, intriguing, handsome—whoa! She couldn't think of him in those terms. No good could or would come of it.

Something brushed her foot and slithered around her ankle. She gave a piercing shriek, shooting up out of the water, scraping her leg on the rocks.

There were no footfalls, but suddenly he was there.

"What the hell is it now?" Marc came up behind her as she stood shivering on the bank. He held a flashlight in one hand and a gun in the other. He played the light on her face.

Heart pounding she squinted into the light. "There's…there's something in the water." She shuddered as the water from her clinging wet hair dripped down her bare legs.

He turned the light on the rippling surface of the pond. An annoying little smile played around the corners of his mouth after he trained the narrow beam into the steaming water. A piece of vine, no more than six inches long, floated just below the surface. "Yeah, I can see how this could scare the hell out of you."

Tory gritted her teeth. How was she supposed to have seen it? Mr. Macho had kept the flashlight with him. She glanced down, she was naked—again—and standing dripping on her neatly folded clothes. With a moan she picked up the damp clothes and hugged them to her chest. "Turn around," she demanded, hot all over.

Marc turned around in a full circle. Directing the full force of his pale eyes on her naked skin. Up and down, down and up. She felt the heat of his gaze like a caress. Her heart stopped, then started beating triple time as he flicked off the flashlight, plunging them into the ethereal, faint sapphire glow from the lake. It illuminated the hard planes of his cheekbones. His eyes glittered dangerously, as he watched her, as if he couldn't help himself.

She could see his body quite clearly in the soft iridescent glow of the water. Which meant he could see her just as clearly—see the trickle of water slowly streaming between her breasts She clutched the clothes tighter to her midriff, until her hand hurt. While she'd never felt it before, this intense, consuming attraction had her ready to explode. Tory felt another trickle of water beading on her breast, and saw his eyes follow its path. Mesmerized, she stood absolutely still, feeling her blood heat and surge through her body.

His muscles flexed under satin-smooth skin. "Princess," he warned in a strange deep tone that made her nerve endings shiver. "Now would be a great time to cut and run." .

He stepped closer, his footsteps muffled on the springy turf surrounding the pool. He was so close she could feel the heat and power of his hard body all the way down her naked torso. His hand came up to push her wet hair back over one shoulder. His touch was gentle, but his voice was harsh. "Run."

"I…can't." If her life depended on it, Tory couldn't have moved right then.

"Tell me to stop."

"I don't want you to stop."

He half chuckled, half groaned. "Drop the clothes, Tory."

The bundle of damp clothing fell to rest near her bare feet. She tilted her face up to look at him.

His finger traced over her lips. "I like your mouth. More than I should."

He drew in a sharp breath as he moved the rest of her long hair over the other shoulder until she stood fully exposed before him. His shadowy eyes swept over her body. She felt strangely euphoric as she saw the rapid rise and fall of his chest just inches away from her.

Involuntarily her own hand reached out to touch the springy mat of hair on his chest. His fingers slipped down her bare arm to hold her hand in place. "Do you know what you're doing?"

She felt the wild tattoo of his heartbeat under her palm, and curled her fingers, brushing her knuckles against muscle and hot skin. An electric sensation shivered up her arm. Her wet hair clung to her back as she swayed closer. "I'm hoping you know enough for both of us."

His mouth found hers, and Tory closed her eyes as she felt him part her lips with the delicious heat of his tongue. A low thrill surged through her body as he kissed her until she was light-headed, his mouth moist and insistent as he urged her to respond.

Marc dragged his mouth away from hers, then claimed her lips again in a series of deep kisses that had her straining on tiptoe against the wall of his chest. She couldn't seem to get close enough.

Taking a handful of her wet hair, he drew it with maddening slowness across her breasts. "If you had any idea…" His voice was thick as he smoothed the strands down her breasts, across the quivering curve of her belly and down. Her hair was cool against her naked skin but she could feel the heat of Marc's fingers through the wet strands. Her skin felt ultrasensitive as his incredibly inventive hands trailed to the very ends of her hair.

His callused fingers dipped fleetingly into the crease between her thighs. Tory thought she might fly out of her skin.

"If you knew what fantasies I've had about your hair…" he whispered.

His hand slid up her narrow rib cage and covered her damp breast. Her nipple was so engorged that it actually hurt, demanding attention. Her body swayed toward him as he smoothed both hands across the aching peaks. Her head felt unbearably heavy and she rested it against his chest. When she opened her mouth against his throat, his hot skin tasted slightly salty, and she could feel the thundering of his heartbeat.

"Tory," he said hoarsely, warningly. She kissed his throat again, passionately.

"Make love to me," she whispered against his skin. "Please, Marc, make love to me." Her cool hands skimmed the small of his back as she tried to pull him even closer.

He wanted to argue that this was neither the time nor the place. It defied logic, that she would feel so incredibly wonderful against him, that her breast fit his hand just right, that her satin skin seemed made for his touch. That she was so perfect.

Perfectly *wrong* for him in every way.

He gritted his teeth as her hand skimmed across his stomach. "Seems as if neither one of us knows what we're doing," Marc muttered, his voice ragged.

Tory felt the muscles under her hand tighten as he hesitated. She felt powerful. Invincible. Gloriously unafraid. She slid her hand down to the waistband of his briefs.

He clutched her wrist and held it away, his mouth coming down on hers in another soul-stealing kiss. Tory pulled her arm free and wrapped it around his sleek muscled back. His body was hard and heavy as he lowered her onto the cool bed of moss.

His mouth, fixed on hers, was greedy, devouring. He seemed to want to absorb her. He kissed her hotly, insistently, and she gave back to him, tasting, savoring the dark flavor of him.

He lowered his mouth to taste one breast and Tory jerked as his hair brushed her skin. The touch of his hot, wet mouth on her breast was electrifying.

She felt the rasp of his teeth on her nipple, and she

arched her back as the hard length of his arousal pressed at the juncture of her thighs. Moaning, she greedily ran her mouth over any part of him she could reach. He tasted so good, she couldn't get enough of him. His skin was like hot satin here, rough there. She savored every new texture.

With his hands, followed by his open mouth, he caressed every exposed part of her—first her thighs, then down the length of her legs until she moved restlessly against him.

Tory's eyes fluttered open as he rose to strip off his briefs. He was fully, magnificently, erect. He knelt down between her legs, his eyes dark, his chest moving rapidly as he sucked in much-needed air. Victoria shivered from the heat of his gaze as he slowly moved his hands to the juncture of her thighs, his concentration frustrating and complete. She wanted him to hurry, but he moved with methodical precision to untangle her long tresses from the nest of short curls at the apex of her thighs. Then, gripping both her arms, he settled them above her head so that she lay suppliant and exposed before him.

"You're perfect." The heat of his pale eyes was like a physical caress as he scrutinized her. But she wanted more. The blanket of wet hair stuck to her skin, tickling nerves already screaming for his touch.

She licked her lips, groaning when he cupped both breasts in his hands. Her aching nipples were soothed momentarily as he took each hard bud between his fingers, rotating them. An instant later, he settled his mouth on one peak, drawing it in, teasing excruciatingly with his tongue. When his hand trailed down over the swell of her hip and brushed through the damp curls she gasped.

He opened her with his fingers, and she felt his first intimate touch. Her body arched reflexively. She cried out as two fingers slipped inside her. Her vision blurred, and she clutched a handful of the sweet-smelling grass above her head.

"Marc?" she whispered.

He stared into her eyes, the tendons in his neck rigid as he groaned through clenched teeth. "God, you're wonderfully responsive." Again his fingers moved inside her, creating a tension that had her moving restlessly, hungrily, against his hand.

She bit her lip as he moved his hands around her to pull her more tightly against him. Her hand tangled in his hair. It felt silky smooth as it skimmed his broad tanned shoulders. A wash of intense emotion gripped her—she wanted to absorb him totally. Parting her lips, she drew in a ragged breath.

Marc rocked his hips against hers. Her body felt swollen and ready to burst as he kept up the steady rhythm.

"Please…" She tightened her fingers in his hair. "Oh, please. I…need you…inside."

He ground the rock-hard ridge of his arousal against her pelvic bone again and again. "You're not ready."

Not ready? Feelings she had no control over shimmered through her body. Her cry, as she climaxed, ricocheted against the cave walls and echoed deep inside her.

Dimly she heard Marc whisper her name as he entered

her. The pain was brief, her need greater. Tory wrapped her legs around his waist, thinking she would die of pleasure. She rose and fell with him as he moved in and out in a maddening rhythm that had her moaning his name.

Her mouth open, wild for his kisses, Tory dug her nails into his back. His hands came down to cup her bottom, lifting her so he could thrust more deeply inside her. Tory caught the edge of the wave, her hips countering his until he stiffened, and with a final thrust, carried them both over the top of a tidal wave.

Tory wrapped her arm around his sweat-drenched back and felt the muscles tense as she held him. She welcomed the heavy weight sprawled on top of her as she struggled to regulate her breathing. She could hear water dripping somewhere in the cave. Marc's breath tickled the side of her neck, cooling her hot skin.

A lump formed in her throat as she caressed his skin, exploring first one ridge of scars, then another. She tried to soothe those long-ago hurts. Emotionally drained as his weight pressed her into the soft sand, she closed her eyes, pretending to be asleep to avoid the cold look he'd give her once he realized what he'd done. Slept with Alex's sister.

Marc was livid. What a dammed idiotic thing for him to have done. He stood, looking down at her, sprawled seductively against the sand and emerald ground cover.

He scrubbed his eyes and then dropped his hand when he smelled her there. "Damn."

Tossing the other blanket over her tempting body, he poured a cup of water and drained it. He'd hauled her unwilling ass here to find her brother. Her brother—his friend. Having sex with her was against the friend code, the T-FLAC operations code, and his own code of ethics. She was a civilian—yet another code, damn it!

Marc rose and pulled on his briefs, keeping his gaze firmly averted from the woman pretending to be asleep. He was dying for a cigarette and he didn't even smoke.

What in the hell was going on here? His training made it possible for him to clear his mind of the sexual fog, although to his annoyance it wasn't that easy.

T-FLAC had been after the terrorist group called Spider for more than seven years. Only after Lynx had gone in undercover had they discovered that two men ran the organization—Samuel Hoag and Christoph Ragno.

Hoag had appeared out of nowhere. No one knew anything about him.

The Spider group was into any illegal activity that offered a quick profit. From Prague to Pretoria the group was small and almost invisible.

But not invincible.

T-FLAC intel had showed that Ragno was a ruthless psychopath. He had been a drug dealer in South America when he'd disappeared several years ago. Before Marc's early retirement he'd been hot on the son of a bitch's trail. In the course of his investigation into Ragno's operation he'd captured a dozen of the tango's key people.

Ragno and T-FLAC had been on each other's hit list for years.

Marc thought about it. Once the tangos connected Lynx to Phantom, they had set the trap. Made sure that the mutilated body of the T-FLAC operative was found by the right people.

There were only three people who knew who Phantom was. Himself, Lynx, and now Victoria Jones. He'd recruited Lynx himself. He'd trained him, and Marc knew without a doubt that nothing, up to and including death, would make his operative turn.

Victoria Jones, on the other hand, had been on the island for two weeks. She was bright enough to have taken what her brother had told her in his letter and with some intelligent thought come up with something damn close to the truth. It wouldn't have taken much for Spider's henchmen to break *her.* Whether she'd meant to or not, there was a good possibility that Tory had given Spider exactly what they wanted—

Him.

Marc picked up the Uzi and headed outside. Heavy rain poured from a charcoal-gray sky. The air smelled fresh and clean. Resting the weapon on his drawn-up leg, he gazed out across the open expanse of rain-tossed ocean. He couldn't remember the last time he'd thought with his balls. He ground his teeth and fingered the trigger of the Uzi.

Angry with himself for succumbing to his desire for her, he wanted to let go and spray the rain with bullets. One of those Alpha male efforts in futility. He wanted someone to come around that corner so that he could pound his fist into their bones and feel their flesh split.

The scent of Victoria Jones had seeped into the membrane of his nostrils, blocking out the smell of ozone. Blocking out common sense. This was not good, not good at all. He had to make sure this didn't happen again. Thinking about her was going to get him killed if he didn't start using a more rational part of his anatomy.

Just how far would she go to save her brother? Stupid question. She'd do anything to ensure his safety. Just for a moment there, when he'd looked down into those clear green eyes, just before he'd buried himself in the warmth of her body, he'd felt a flicker of emotion. Which just went to show what an idiot he was.

What he had to do was confront her, not screw her. They would both be safer that way. She was already nervous as hell around him, hell, he'd done everything he could to scare her back in Montana. Why wouldn't she be scared of him? Fine. If he made her nervous she'd back off if he made another advance...

Damn. He rubbed his hand over his face. He was putting the onus of abstinence on the shoulders of the very woman whose body he lusted after. He'd lost his frigging mind.

He heard her coming long before she spoke.

"What are you doing out here?"

She was wearing one of his black T-shirts which hit her midthigh and left the mouthwatering length of her pale slender legs bare. He knew damn well she was naked underneath. Her small breasts molded the thin cotton. He steeled himself. This was do-or-die time. He pressed the ugly mouth of the gun between her breasts.

Tory's eyes widened. The delectable, pale pink lips curved into a tentative smile. "I'm sorry," she whispered huskily. "I didn't mean to scare you."

Marc hardened his heart and forced the rest of his

body to relax. "You scare me, all right, honey, but not in the way you think." He lowered the Uzi. He turned away to look out at the churning ocean. He felt her tentative touch on his bare arm and shrugged it away. "Go back to camp."

"Are you coming to bed soon?"

"Thanks, but no thanks." His voice was flat. "I've had my sex for tonight." Marc hitched his bare foot on the rock behind him and rested the gun on his knee.

She frowned, confused. "Wh—why?"

He could give her a long list of nasty answers. "Spit it out, honey." A wave shot thirty feet in the air in a burst of white spume. "Why what?"

"Why are you talking to me like this?"

Marc turned to look at her. There was a crease of confusion between her brows and she was biting her lower lip. *Make it good, pal.* "You think because I took your virginity I should give you a promise and a ring? Get a life, lady. Sex is sex."

Her hand flashed out with surprising speed, connecting with his cheek. His face stung. He deserved a hell of a lot more than a slap on the cheek from her. He narrowed his eyes and gave her his meanest, get the fuck out of my way look. "Don't ever hit unless you expect to be hit back." He kept his eyes cold "You seem to be under the mistaken belief that I'm a gentleman. I'm not."

"No one," Tory countered, "would ever mistake you for anything other than what you are." Her cheeks flamed with obvious fury. "You're hard and cruel and a…a bully. Why don't you go ahead and hit me back? Maybe it would make you feel more like a man."

"Don't tempt me," he said tightly, leaning against the rock, the marks of her fingers a burning brand on his face.

"You're despicable." He saw the way her hand trembled as she suddenly realized that he was aroused. Her eyes shot from his erection to his face and stayed there, her cheeks scarlet.

"Despicable? Lady, you ain't seen nothing yet." He laughed unpleasantly. *Tell me what a prick I am, and walk away Victoria Jones ex-virgin. Just fucking walk away while the going is good.* Her eyes flashed, and her soft pink lips, still slightly swollen from his kisses, tightened. He rubbed at the raised scar on his shoulder—just to remind himself.

Then she made the fatal mistake of tilting her chin at him. With a smoothness that belied his jerking pulse, he pulled her hard against him. "You liked it." He looked down at her tense face. "Is that it, baby? You want more?" He trailed his hand down the damp satin of her hair, pulling her hips into the cradle of his own with a jerk that caught her off balance.

He kissed her hard, roughly forcing her mouth open and thrusting his tongue into the remembered sweetness. She tried to close her mouth and he used his free hand to squeeze her jaw. The other hand pressed her more tightly against his arousal.

"Like that? Is this what you want? Does it turn you on to know that just looking at you makes me hard?" *Kick me in the nuts, damn it.* Where the hell was her self-preservation? She struggled in his arms. "Let… me…go!"

He let her go with a suddenness that surprised them both. She rubbed her arm over her swollen mouth and glared at him. "Don't ever come near me again—except to save my brother, which was my focus and the reason you dragged me here in the first place." Her voice was rock steady.

The fact that she was behaving exactly as he wanted her to pissed him off. Christ. She was turning him into an emotional pretzel. Marc picked up the gun he'd dropped and pulled out the clip to check for sand. He looked at her over his shoulder. "Was it worth losing your virginity to save your precious brother?" The metallic clink as he snapped the clip back couldn't smother the sound of her gasp.

"It wasn't like that," she said furiously, stepping toward him.

Anger and resentment flared through him—how easily she got under his skin and past his defenses. "I'll give you ten seconds to get your butt back to camp." He said it coldly, his gaze running the length of her legs, then lifting to focus on the rapid rise and fall of her breasts.

"All I want to know—"

"Three."

"—is why you're—"

"Four."

"Stop count—"

"Five."

"Stop doing that! Tell me what I—"

"Seven. Eight. Nine. Go!" Marc cocked the gun and pointed it at her heart. She wasn't afraid of the damned gun, but her eyes widened as she saw what was in his eyes.

She ran.

# CHAPTER SEVEN

SHAKING WITH THE RUSH of adrenaline, Tory pulled on bra, panties and borrowed clothes with jerky movements. If she had a flak vest she would have pulled that on, too. Her teeth were clenched so hard her jaw hurt. Anger, confusion and embarrassment made her stomach churn.

"Don't yell at me, you—you…*Neanderthal!*" She was pretty brave when there wasn't anyone listening. She wasn't used to being yelled at. Other than on the subject of Alex, there'd never been an argument in her home. Certainly there'd never been a raised voice, never a clash of opinion. A shy, quiet child to begin with, she'd been so afraid her grandmother would send her away as she'd done with Alex, that Tory had toed the line with no complaint. Even to herself.

*As for being touched,* she thought with annoyance. *Touched?* Marc Savin didn't just *touch*. He *manhandled.* He grabbed, he stroked, he fondled. The man put his big hands on her whenever he felt the urge, and she resented him for it. Especially if he was going to react like *that* about it afterward.

She had no frame of reference, but their lovemaking had been nothing short of spectacular. Apparently it had only been spectacular for *her*. "Rude, irrational...*jerk*."

Her wrist ached. Her ribs hurt. But the most uncomfortable injury was her bruised ego. And she guessed her arm would heal long before her heart knitted back to normal. She tried to rationalize his sudden anger. After thirty seconds she gave up. It made no sense whatsoever. Not only did it not make sense after what they'd shared, there was no point trying to interpret the male mind.

She was tired of being scared spitless. Tired of feeling off balance. Tired of fitting like a square peg in a round-hole situation.

She liked *quiet*.

She liked every day to be exactly the same as the day before.

Boring was good.

Boring was comfortable.

She *liked* boring.

"No, I *love* boring."

Being around Marc Savin was anything but boring. Being around him was like being stuck on a roller-coaster ride without a safety strap.

"It's not as though I *asked* to come here," she muttered crossly as she prepared a pot of coffee, just enough for one. "*He* was the one who dragged me willy-nilly across the world, against my protests." She searched for a mug. "I *told* him he'd be sorry. I *told* him I wasn't terribly brave." She paused. "He got *sex*. So what is he so blasted cranky about?"

It might not be in her grandmother's book of etiquette, but the son of a bitch had *deserved* that slap.

She should have known better. She *did* know better. Except that making love with Marc had seemed so inevitably *right*.

He'd intentionally made her angry, she was sure—*pretty* sure. Or maybe he was one of those men who didn't want the woman to get "ideas" after sex. As if she would. Their lives would never mesh. Of *course* they had no future.

Yet when he'd been making love to her he'd been gentle and affectionate. Could he have faked that? Probably. But had he? Tory frowned. There had been no need to pretend. She'd been willing—more than willing, to make love with him. He hadn't needed to whisper sweet words to her. He hadn't needed to spend as much time as he had on foreplay, she thought as her cheeks heated.

*I'm trying to romanticize what was just a man scratching an itch. But let's say,* she thought, *let's say he was really into making love to me. Not just a body, but me, Victoria Jones.* Then he remembered that he was here to search for one of his operatives. A man he considered a friend. He was on assignment, or whatever it was called. His friend was in danger. His hands were tied because he couldn't search in the daylight hours, and there were a lot of daylight hours to fill while he waited.

Sex was good, but he didn't want to have his friend's sister mooning over him for the duration. He had to make sure said woman didn't get the wrong idea. He knew she was afraid of her own shadow. It wouldn't, *hadn't,* been hard to scare her away. This time her face flushed with embarrassment instead of heating with the memory of his hands on her skin.

The scenario made some kind of convoluted sense. At least she'd gone through some logical steps to arrive at some sort of explanation. It would have to do.

The coffee was ready and she poured every drop into a mug. He was rude. Uncommunicative. Hostile… "Really, a person would need a thesaurus." Irrational. A tender, wonderfully considerate lover—

"Talking to yourself?"

Startled, Tory spun around. "Yes. And it was a rational, intelligent conversation."

He eyed her coffee mug. "Is that for me?"

"Dream on," she told him daringly, then sipped her coffee while giving him a cool look over the rim. "Why are you always so surly?" He hadn't been the least bit unpleasant when they'd made love earlier. But perhaps that was because his mouth had been busy. Her heart skittered and she concentrated on swallowing.

"Welcome to the real world. You're just too sheltered to play in the big leagues."

"I'd like to point out that I didn't want to play in *any* league, let alone the rude league." She kept her attention on his face, trying not to be distracted by his impressive physique. He was hard and firm, and she knew, smooth to the touch. "You were the dragger." Her mouth went dry, but she couldn't look away. "I was the *dragee.*"

His lips twitched, but he poured water and coffee into the pot and turned up the flame without comment.

She might not like his methods, but she reminded

herself that she did trust him to find Alex, *and* to keep them all safe until he got them home. "May I suggest you put on some clothes before you burn—something important?"

"Christ, woman, you belong in another century," he muttered, pulling on his clothes—black of course. Dressed, he sat on the sandy floor to lace up his boots.

Clearly the idea that she was so out of step with his definition of what was appropriate ticked him off. Too bad. "And *this* is what set you off like a lunatic out there?" Speaking her mind felt wonderful. Liberating.

She almost jumped out of her skin when he laughed. It sounded rusty, but it *was* a short soft laugh. "I thought you were a coward?"

Tory swallowed. She couldn't believe that had just popped out of her mouth. Being defiant in her mind was one thing. Blurting it out quite another. "Believe me, I am."

"I know this'll come as a hell of a shock," he said drily, getting up to fill his cup. "But some of the worst tangos—terrorists—in the world used to be shit scared of me."

Clearly he'd like her to feel the same way. "I'm very happy to hear it. I hope they still are since many of them live here on Marezzo, and you're going to have to go through them to get Alex."

"Don't get too—" He stopped abruptly, putting up a hand to silence her. In one smooth motion he picked up the big gun he'd had outside. Motioning her back into the shadows, he handed her the Uzi. Her eyes went wide as she felt the unfamiliar weight and texture of the weapon in her hand. It was unwieldy with the cast on one arm, but Marc positioned it with quick efficiency.

"It's ready to go," he said so quietly she was amazed she could hear him at all. "Shoot the first person that comes around that corner. No questions."

In a blink he was gone.

COULD BE KIDS EXPLORING, Marc thought, keeping his weapon raised as he listened for the soft whisper of footsteps on sand coming from the other chamber of the cave. Could be one of the Spiders crawling around looking for the fly they'd invited into their web. He hoped it was the latter. Beating the shit out of something that could fight back would be just fucking great right about now.

His ploy had backfired. So much for *that* brilliant idea. Hopefully he'd retrieve her brother in the next couple of hours and get them to the mainland. Then he wouldn't need to come up with asinine, unworkable plans to keep her at arm's length.

*Bring it on.*

Whoever these guys were they didn't want to be heard.

Not kids. Not locals, either. These guys knew how to walk silently across the gritty rocks. They weren't chatting. Hell, they were barely breathing. He sensed them more than heard them. Their very stealth indicated an awareness that someone else—him—was in the caves.

A pleasant surge of adrenaline reminded Marc of how much he used to love his job. Of how badly he'd missed *this* in the three years of his retirement.

Scaling a low rock wall, he leaped lightly from there

up onto a ledge he'd discovered earlier. The ledge ran nine or ten feet off the ground, and was less then twelve inches wide in some places, but it ran for a good two hundred feet around the south side of the main cavern.

Shifting ripples of silver reflected off the deep turquoise water, bouncing off the rock and his black-clad body. A convenient camouflage as he stalked his prey.

It wasn't long before he caught up with them.

Three men.

Disappointing.

He waited for the right moment to take them out. They split up to skirt the small lake. Two on the opposite side, one, conveniently, almost directly below the ledge.

After holstering the Walther to free up his hands, Marc dropped soundlessly behind the guy, snapping his neck before he was even aware he wasn't alone.

One down. Two to go.

Leaving the body on the sand, he caught up with the others in a narrow area not conducive to firing a weapon. Bullets had a tendency to ricochet. He pulled out the Ka-bar.

The men had to go single file through the opening. Hell, Marc thought coming up behind them, this was like shooting fish in a barrel. He needed a challenge for his rusty skills and these yahoos were practically handing themselves to him on a silver platter.

He wrapped his forearm around the man's throat, jerking him off balance as he stuck the knife up high in his kidneys. It was a swift death. And silent.

Two down. One to go.

Oblivious, the man in front had moved twenty paces ahead, but he turned, perhaps to say something to his partner, possibly because he'd heard the sound of the body dropping.

*"Figlio di Gotta!"* After a nanosecond of shock, he remembered he had a weapon in his hand—a Ruger 9mm—and probably figured now would be a great time to take aim.

*"Fessacchione!"* One shot and the bullet could take them both out. He watched the guy's eyes—mere glints in the semidarkness to see if he really was stupid enough to fire.

*"Baciami il culo!"*

"Yours isn't the ass I want to kiss," Marc assured him as he flung the Ka-bar. It turned blade over hilt in a glittering arc, then struck the man in the throat. Blood spurted from his jugular. His eyes went wide. The Ruger discharged as he crumpled to the ground. Marc threw himself down as the shot went wild, bouncing off the stone walls like the pinball in a video game.

After zigging and zagging unpredictably the bullet imbedded itself in the rock a foot from Marc's left shoulder.

Three for three.

He dragged each man to the lake, and the whirlpool that indicated the tunnel that drained out into the ocean. Nature's garbage disposal, he thought, feeding the bodies into the vortex. In seconds each body disappeared.

And Marc was back to being alone with the woman he most wanted to avoid.

"It's me," he said before rounding the corner. He

didn't doubt for a moment that Tory would shoot as instructed. The Uzi wasn't that discriminating. Even a bad shot could hit a target eventually.

"Identify yourself."

"You have a birthmark under your left breast."

"Your name would have been sufficient," she told him without moving. Her lashes flicked as she looked down at the Uzi braced on her hip. Her fingers were white with tension. "Would you please take this thing?"

Marc clicked on the safety, then took the weapon from her.

"Put it down," she instructed quietly. He shot her a glance.

"Now."

He set the Uzi near the pack, ready if he needed it. He'd barely straightened, when, without warning, Tory flung herself into his arms. "I heard the shot. I was so worried you'd been hurt!

Her cheek was damp against his throat. Marc smiled as he cradled the back of her head in his palm. He could feel the syncopation of her heart against his chest. "So little faith, princess?"

She pulled away. Face pale, she ran cold hands across his chest and over his arms. "Were you hit?"

Marc bracketed her face and kissed her.

Tory choked back a sob as he fitted his mouth over hers. She'd been terrified. The blast of a single shot still fresh in her mind. Deathly frightened by the prolonged silence as she stood there in the semidarkness, the nasty weapon gripped in her good hand, her heart beating in her ears. Listening. Waiting. Praying.

At the sound of gunfire, she'd almost cried out, biting her tongue so as not to give away her position. She couldn't begin to imagine what was going on out there, but she was certain that at any second a man would appear in the entrance to their camp and shoot her on sight. Conversely, being shot would have been a blessing. She'd already had one run-in with these people and she didn't relish the idea of a repeat performance.

Marc's mouth was hot and wild on hers, and Tory couldn't help but respond to the urgency in his kiss. Her tears made the kiss salty. He tangled his fingers in her hair, drawing her more tightly against his body. His mouth softened on hers.

"I've never met a woman like you," he said quietly. With barely exerted pressure he pulled her down beside him onto the sand. It wasn't difficult. It was where she wanted to be.

She looked up at his face looming above her. The hard line of his jaw was blurred under the dark, bristly shadow of several day's growth of beard. His pale eyes glittered as he wiped her wet cheeks with his thumb. "You know you're out of your league here, right?"

"My league? I keep telling you I don't have one. But if you're talking about my lack of sexual experience, that was a choice, one I'm proud of."

"Yeah. I know. I was there. But you shouldn't have chosen me. All that did was add another thing to my list of demerits."

Her heart tripped. "I'm not keeping a running tally."

"You should. God help you, you really should."

"This is a unique situation. Let's enjoy it while it lasts." Her arm circled his neck as his head blocked out the sapphire glow from the lake in the next cavern.

His lips touched hers—softly, gently. Tory found her fingers tightening in the thick hair at his nape; as if in response, his lips moved more insistently on hers and his tongue invaded her mouth. She closed her eyes as sensation washed over her. Her T-shirt was up around her throat, her bra loose and hanging, as her breasts were pressed flat against the hard wall of his chest.

She felt the pounding of his heart beating in perfect rhythm with her own. Her skin felt alive as he drew his hand under her head and swept her hair out of the way. It would be full of sand, but she didn't care. "You're pure hell on my good intentions—you know that, princess?" He lifted his head to look down at her. He caressed her bottom lip with his thumb, his eyes locked with hers.

Tory tentatively tasted his skin with the tip of her tongue. His pupils flared. She took a little nip from his thumb and he retaliated by crushing her to him, devouring her mouth until she was weak.

He kissed her with an intensity and dedication that would have awed her if she'd been in her right mind. When he eventually broke the kiss they were both breathing hard. Then his clever lips moved down her throat and she felt the shocking wet heat of his open mouth on her nipple. She kneaded the damp skin of his back as he lavished his attention first on one hard peak and then the other. Tory realized that she was making small insistent noises in the back of her throat. He wouldn't be hurried, though. With slow thoroughness his mouth moved down her rib cage. Her skin was on fire as his fingers opened her, and as predictably as a sunrise his mouth found her. She couldn't help herself; her legs moved restlessly under the onslaught as his lips and tongue brought her right to the edge.

She wanted him. Now. "Marc…please, oh, please…" She clutched at his hair until he moved back up her body and settled into the cradle of her thighs. He surged into her and her climax came forcefully and immediately.

He held her in the harbor of his strong arms until the shudders that racked her body died away. And then he started to move again as if he'd never stopped.

Tory's head thrashed in the sand. "No…more… I can't…"

But she realized with amazement that she could, when she felt his powerful hands grip her bottom and his steady thrust become harder, faster, deeper.

"Come with me, sweetheart. Come with me." His voice was harsh in her ear, as he drove into her again and again.

"Yes… Like that…" He inhaled sharply as her hips rose, then she felt his hands slide under her as he clutched her bottom, showing her how to move. "God! Yes…yes…!"

Astounded she felt her muscles gather and tense, and when he gave one last surge, his shout was echoed by hers.

Her body tightened and soared, then dissolved in a heap beneath him as he collapsed against her, his breath ragged against her throat.

Her hair had been tossed about and Marc moved a strand from where it stuck to her hot, damp cheek. "You're so beautiful," he murmured. His hand lingered on her face as he looked down at her with a slightly bemused expression. "When I look at you, all I can think about are clean sheets on a big bed."

"We seem to have done all right on the ground," Tory said shyly, smoothing the frown between his eyes with one finger.

He took her hand from his face and kissed her fingertips before rolling onto his back, taking her with him. Her chin rested on his chest where his heart still beat an excited tattoo.

Turning her head so his chest pillowed her cheek, Tory smoothed her hand down the hard flat muscles, playing with the crisp dark hairs. She felt his lips against her hair. "Talk to me," he said.

Perfectly relaxed and content in the semidarkness, Tory complied. She told him how, when she'd been a young child, her grandmother had been a night nurse, and the house had always been closed up and dark during the day so that the woman could sleep. She told him of her heartache over her grandmother's refusal to adopt Alex or allow him to visit his sister.

Tory said little about her bookkeeping job and skirted around his question about whom she'd dated. Her grandmother had refused to allow her the usual freedoms granted most teenagers and by the time she'd died and Tory was living on her own, she'd felt painfully out of sync with the men she met.

She nuzzled closer, blissfully happy. In a few hours

he'd leave to go out and look for her brother. When the two men returned it would be time to say goodbye. She was going to treasure every second with him until then.

## CHAPTER EIGHT

"HAVE YOU EVER BEEN in love?" Tory asked softly. Sprawled bonelessly over his body she nuzzled her mouth against the underside of his jaw.

She hadn't gone for the hard sell; he might as well give the soft-shoe shuffle a shot, Marc thought drily. But he couldn't resist stroking her back beneath the silky skeins of her long hair. "I'm not a stick-around kind of guy. You might have guessed that by now." How could skin be this soft? This sensitive? How could she smell of vanilla after all she'd been through in the last few days?

"Why not?" She traced a path along his jawline with her damp mouth, her fingers tangled in his hair. He liked the weight of her blanketed over his body. He enjoyed the feel of her slender hands petting him.

"Too many people I cared about have—" *Betrayed me,* he thought, and replaced it with "—been taken away from me. I just don't trust the hell out of fate."

"What if I trust it enough for both of us?" Her mouth was beside his ear now, and her warm breath made him shudder with every soft word.

*Then I'd call you a fool,* he thought grimly. "Don't

delude yourself, I'm not capable. I've seen too much to ever have the naive belief that love will conquer all. Any excess emotion makes a man weak, be it love or hate. I can't afford to be off guard. My life and those of my colleagues depend on my having a clear head."

He missed his T-FLAC operatives. He missed the life that had once been his world. Guilt still ate at him that he'd allowed Alex Stone to come here to Marezzo alone. Whiling away the useless hours before dawn with his friend's sister wasn't exactly a stellar move. Another rock in his suitcase of guilt.

He seemed to be compounding it stone by stone.

Tory cupped his cheek in her cool palm and brushed her mouth over his as delicately as a butterfly's wing. "And an empty heart?"

Yeah. It probably would be empty. If he had one. He didn't. Made life a hell of a lot easier to deal with that way. He tilted her chin up so that her eyes met his, needing her to understand just a little. "I want you more than I've ever wanted another woman—if that means anything." It shocked him to realize that he spoke the truth.

"Does it to you?" she asked wistfully.

"Yes." His mouth was less than a whisper away as he breathed the words like a prayer, "Yes, God help me. It's all I've got to give."

"Who hurt you, Marc? What woman made you lose the ability to love?"

"What makes you think there was a woman?" *What makes you think I was ever capable of giving or receiving love?*

Tory regarded him steadily in the rippling glow from the distant lake. Her eyes were very green, very serious. She brushed her hand across his shoulder. "Because I know that someone hurt you very badly. Because sometimes when you look at me, and I can see how much you want me, you rub at this scar right here and the heat goes out of your eyes and you try to make me hate you."

Marc eased her down against his chest so she wasn't looking at him with rainwater-clear eyes and a mouth made for his kisses. "I shouldn't have to convince you to stay away from me, Tory. I'm a man. I'll take whatever you offer me. Sex doesn't have to mean anything."

"Okay. I get it," she said without heat. "What was her name?"

"Krista Davis." He waited for that dark hole to open up inside him. He waited... But the darkness that always came when he thought of Krista's laugh didn't materialize.

"Blue eyes, silky blond hair," Tory guessed. "A chest out to there. A petite Barbie doll who could probably shoot a gun beside you all day and then be home in time to cook a gourmet dinner. Probably wearing a black negligee. Every man's fantasy—lucky you."

"Ever heard the expression, 'Be careful what you wish for'?"

"My grandmother said it all the time. I learned early to keep my 'wishes' few and far between. And realistic." When he tightened his arms around her she prodded him with her chin. "Go on."

He glanced at his wristwatch. Half an hour until he figured it was safe to go out. Safe was a relative term. Safe normally entailed stealthily moving unnoticed in the darkness, but apparently Tory's special sensory gift required a minimal amount of light for clarity. Half an hour of pillow talk wouldn't kill him. Would it? And it would keep his mind off the risky daylight assault ahead of them.

"I recruited and trained Krista myself. She was one of my best operatives. God, she was quick as lightning. She would size up a situation and handle it before any of my other people had even realized that there might be a problem. She was absolutely fearless. Afraid of nothing."

*Bully for her. Courage and cleavage.* "I don't need to know the details," Tory said tightly. "Just hit the high points."

"We worked together on several jobs. She was an excellent shot, I trusted her with my life." They'd been lovers for a year. Krista had been pushing to get married, even knowing that operatives rarely married, and even more rarely married fellow T-FLAC operatives.

The more Krista pressed, the more Marc had started believing that he *could* have it all. A job he loved, and also a wife and family. He'd liked the idea of having someone to come home to. Kids… It had been a pipe dream, of course.

"I was down in Mexico City. I'd been undercover for seven months. Everything was copacetic until Krista arrived on the scene.

"'Backup,' she told me. She played her damn part too well. I believed her. She betrayed me. The mission was scrubbed." Not just the mission, but their relationship had changed in his absence. How could it not? *That* he could have lived with. It was what happened later that had changed everything.

"Not all women are like that," Tory murmured. She laid her cheek against his, then pressed closer, wanting to absorb his pain. Tears stung her eyes.

"Krista isn't like that anymore, either. She's dead. But I'll never let anyone else that close again." His voice was cold.

"Did you love her?"

"It was a close facsimile. I told you not to get ideas. Sex is all I can offer you. Take it or leave it."

She met his gaze with a clear-eyed look that went to his heart like a laser. "I'll take it."

"CAN YOU SENSE Alex from here?" Marc asked, wishing he could leave her in the caves. But he had two damn good reasons to keep her close. Alex. And the three men he'd killed probably had buddies who'd soon come looking for them.

"It depends…"

"On?" He checked each weapon and grabbed several packs of ammo.

"On how strong he is." Tory turned her back and indicated her hair. He combed his fingers through it, then tightly braided it. "On if he's conscious. On…I don't know. I sensed he'd been in that house this morning. But I didn't pick up a location. I understand that you'd rather I stay here. But if we want to find him *fast,* you know I'm going to have to go out with you again."

Tucking her braid down inside the back of her T-shirt as he'd done the last time, Marc knew she was right. He didn't like it, goddamn it, but Tory was going to *have* to accompany him again. Shit. "Make sure no one gets a look at this hair. It's too damned memorable." He found a baseball cap stuffed in a side pocket of his pack and pulled it down low over her eyes. "That should do it."

"Pavina?"

"Yeah."

"I spent a couple of hours there last time I was here. I didn't sense Alex there so I headed straight for Pescarna." She pushed the bill of the cap out of her eyes. "It must be ten miles if not more to Pavina. Surely we're not going to walk?"

"If you weren't with me I would." Crouching down, he opened the A.L.I.C.E. pack. "What the hell were you doing messing around in this pack? Damn it woman, I can't find anything!"

"Everything is where it's supposed to be. I had to find the first-aid kit."

"It was right on top." He started pulling things out of the pack and tossing them on the sand. "Don't start nesting, for God's sake."

"I tidied it," she said, striving for lightness. She could see that he was spoiling for a fight—again.

"Leave my things the hell alone."

"Would you listen to yourself? Why are you suddenly so angry?"

"I don't like people messing with my gear. I know where everything is and I—"

"Fine." Tory picked up the plates and got to her feet. "Why don't I just let you rant and rave in private while I go and wash the coffee mugs?"

When she got back, he was tucking his pant legs into the tops of his boots. His hair had been tied back and he had a gun in his hand.

"Are you planning to shoot someone?" Tory asked, giving him a wary glance.

Marc closed his eyes briefly, then lifted his shirt to tuck the Walther into his waistband at the small of his back. His pale eyes assessed her and his mouth tightened. "You can't go out with the cast showing. People will see you a mile away and they'll remember you."

He looked very tall and menacing as he strode across the sand toward her. She moved her feet slightly apart and tilted her chin. She was getting sick and tired of him sniping and snarling at her.

He had something in his hand, but she couldn't see what it was. Tory held her ground as he came right up to her. He looked like a desperado with his earring flashing and dark stubble shadowing his face.

The smile was gone as he said briskly, "Lift your arms."

If he thought for one second that she was going to kiss him, he had another think coming. "Why should I?" she asked belligerently, then recoiled when she saw what he was holding. The blood drained down to her toes. "I hope for your sake that you don't plan on using that belt on *me*." She saw a flash of another man, strap raised…. Her muscles tensed. Until a few weeks ago she'd never had anyone show any form of violence toward her. She'd sworn never to allow herself to be in that situation again.

Yet here she was. Back where the most horrendous hours of her life had been endured. Back in Marezzo. God help her.

*Marc Savin* help her.

Marc gave her one of his wicked smiles, and she forgot everything in the heat of his pewter gaze. "Have you ever thought about being tied up while someone makes love to you, princess?" The loop of the belt came up and stroked her cheek.

She shivered as the smooth leather skimmed down her bare throat. "N-no," she whispered, her voice shaking. "You—you know I haven't." The hard leather belt brushed her nipple through her T-shirt and Tory almost bit off her tongue.

Her eyes locked with his as he caressed her with the belt. She couldn't tell from his expression whether he intended to make love to her again, or if he was just using this as another means to taunt her.

"S-stop that!" She stepped back, away from the unfamiliar and highly erotic feel of the leather.

Marc's hand stilled as he shook his head slightly.

"Just put it on."

Tory snatched it out of his hand and tugged it around her waist, cinching it tightly. He brushed her hands aside and tugged the shirt out to cover it. That done to his satisfaction, he grabbed another black shirt and started ripping it to shreds.

He then wrapped her cast in the fabric. "That should do it. I wish I could cut the frigging thing off."

"What? My arm?" She matched his sarcasm, pulling the bill of her cap lower to hide her face.

"That cast is a liability." Marc finished repacking and dragged the pack into the shadows against the back wall, then stripped everything from the shelf and shoved that into the shadows, too.

"I'm not exactly enjoying being incapacitated, but the cast stays until the doctor says it comes off."

"Does it still hurt?"

"Only when I laugh," she said with a small smile. "It's bearable. Are we ready to go?" She watched as he crammed a lethal-looking knife into the back of his jeans and pulled his shirt down to cover it. He glanced around to see if he'd missed anything.

The belt scratched her bare skin. "I don't need a belt with these jeans."

"You need this belt. It might save your life."

Tory sighed. "Are you going to let me in on this little 'agent' secret or am I going to have to improvise when something happens? What does this belt do, anyway? Make me into a kung fu expert?"

"I'll keep you informed on a need-to-know basis."

"I need to know now."

Marc filled a flask from the collapsible water bottle and clipped it to his belt. "Ready?"

"Let's just go. The sooner we find Alex, the sooner I can get back to my life." She followed him out of camp, speaking to his back. "You know what real life is, don't you? That's where people have what's called conversation. That's where civilized people stay in one mood for more than half an hour. That's where people don't go around with who-knows-what wrapped around their waists."

She impatiently pushed a fern frond out of her way. "There'd better not be the makings of a bomb or anything like that in this stupid belt."

Marc kept walking, moving quickly ahead of her toward the entrance of the cave. "Scared I'll blow you to kingdom come, princess?"

"Nothing you could do would surprise me anymore." She blinked as they emerged from the opening, drawing in deep lungfuls of salty fresh air.

The sky was tinted a pale lavender, the sun just peeking over the horizon in a faint apricot streak. The ocean lay calm and flat like a giant piece of Venetian glass, gilded by the rising sun.

Tory accepted his help down the rocks to the damp sand below. This time, instead of turning right toward Pescarna they headed left, keeping close to the base of the towering limestone cliff.

The few bites of "breakfast" formed a tight knot in Tory's stomach as she hurried to catch up with him. By the time they reached Pavina there would be people all over the place. Tory shivered. Marc had been right. If just one person recognized her from before, their cover would be blown. Nervously she tugged the T-shirt down in back, feeling the reassuring weight of her braid against her bare skin.

Marc turned to watch her scramble over the rocks partially buried in the sand. "Get a move on. I want to get there in time to blend in with the crowds at the market."

He slowed his stride enough so that Tory only had to trot to keep up with him. The cast on her arm was getting heavier by the minute. And despite what she'd told him, her arm ached and the cast chafed and itched her skin.

"Are you going to make it?"

There was no way she could walk one more step on wet sand, where each step weighed ten tons. He was standing waiting for her reply. Tory tilted her chin. "Of course, I'm going to make it. Lead on."

By the time they reached the end of the high cliff she was panting, and her shirt stuck uncomfortably to her back. Marc moved beneath the shadow of a solitary tree that stood on the low bluff, and unclipped the water bottle from his belt. He uncapped it and handed it to her. "Stay here and rest. I'm going to find some transportation." He vanished over the rise and Tory sank down, hugging her knees to her chest and resting her head on her arm.

She wasn't cut out for this cloak-and-dagger stuff. Marc took this all in his stride. Nice for him. She wanted her brother back. She wanted to return to civilization and a real bed. She wanted real food and a knife and fork. She wanted her nice predictable spreadsheets and ledgers. She wanted to meet a nice, ordinary, rational man.

Tory lifted her head and picked up the canvas-covered bottle. The water was lukewarm and tasted slightly of sulfur, but her mouth was parched and she drank greedily before recapping the container and setting it upright in the sand beside her.

The sun was a glorious persimmon ball above the horizon by the time Marc came back. He was wearing a beige linen jacket over his black T-shirt and jeans. The unstructured, creased linen jacket should have looked ridiculous, but instead he looked as though he'd just stepped out of *GQ*. He'd pushed the sleeves up to expose darkly tanned muscular forearms, and there was absolutely no evidence of the arsenal he carried on his body.

"I was in luck. Come on." He pulled her to her feet and attached the bottle to his belt. "I found a farmer who was willing to part with his truck. We'll be in Pavina in about thirty minutes."

He took her hand to pull her up the sandy incline, letting go as soon as they reached flat ground. The truck was parked under a small stand of orange trees. The vehicle looked as if it had survived several wars. It might have been blue, but whatever color it had once been was almost obliterated by rust and pale gray primer.

Tory looked at the vehicle dubiously before climbing into the cab, pushing away debris with her feet. The owner had eaten several weeks' worth of breakfasts, lunches and dinners there by the look and smell of the papers and containers on the floor and seat. She wrinkled her nose as Marc got in. He had to slam his door twice before it closed.

The windows didn't open and the smell of garlic and cheap wine was overpowering. The sun beat in on her side. Marc turned the truck with a spray of sand and headed down the dirt road.

To the right she could see the high flat peak of Monte Tolaro, an extinct volcano rising thousands of feet into the clear blue sky. Marc turned onto a tarred road and headed west toward Pavina. He relaxed in the vinyl seat, one hand on the wheel, the other resting alongside the window. He glanced at her out of the corner of his eye. Tory kept her face turned toward the vineyards that flashed by.

"What will we do when we find Alex?" She pinched a tomato-encrusted paper between her fingers and tossed it behind the seat as she turned more fully to face him.

"When we know exactly where he is, you take the truck back to where I picked you up and go to the grotto and wait for us. As soon as Lynx and I get back, I'll contact Angelo and we're outta here."

"You make it sound so simple." She gazed intensely at him. "But it won't be. Will it?" Her throat tightened and she had to wait for the threat of tears to pass. "They're holding him somewhere and he's badly hurt."

Marc reached out and linked his fingers with hers on her knee. "He's trained for just such an eventuality, Tory. Trust me, I'll get your brother out."

Tory clenched her fingers within the safe harbor of his hand. "Promise?"

Marc squeezed once and then let go to have both hands on the steering wheel as the truck's bald tires fought for purchase on the cobblestones. "Promise."

She believed him. God help her, she did believe he would get Alex out and away safely. The way he treated her was incidental to him saving her brother.

Marc pulled the old pickup in between an open-sided wagon piled high with oranges and a big truck that had a bottle of wine crudely painted on the side.

He put his hand on her shoulder as she moved to open the door.

"Remember, we're just a couple of tourists interested in market day." He removed the gun and checked it under cover of the cracked dashboard. Pulling the key out of the ignition, he handed it to her.

"I want you to stay as close to me as you can." His eyes scanned her pale face. "You'll do fine. The moment you know where they're holding Alex, just let me know. Walk slowly, look around. And for God's sake," he warned lightly, "don't look so terrified."

"I am terrified. What if…?"

He kissed her—just pulled her toward him and locked his arms around her and kissed her hard. It was a kiss totally unlike any of the others. His mouth scorched hers, his arms were like a vise around her and she could feel her heart pounding in her ears. The heady, familiar scent of him made her mouth relax under his.

When he lifted his mouth from hers she wanted to beg him for just one more, but the key dug into the tender flesh of her palm.

He leaned back against the seat and said with satisfaction, "We were being watched. That should do it."

"You…you kissed me like that because someone was watching us?"

Marc adjusted his jacket, checking to make sure his weapons didn't show. "It's called a cover, princess."

Furious, she forgot to be scared. She started to put the key in her front pocket.

Marc plucked the key out of her hand and hid it

under his seat. "Leave it here in the truck. If for some reason we become separated, get your ass back here and get the hell out of here. Got it?"

# CHAPTER NINE

THEY WERE JOSTLED by hordes of people moving through the enormous gates of the walled city of Pavina. No vehicular traffic was allowed in, and the narrow cobbled streets were crowded with pedestrians. Tory pressed up against Marc as they allowed the momentum of the crowd to push them toward the piazza, where the weekly market was in full swing.

The scent of oranges, garlic, hot sweaty bodies and wine filled the air, and she breathed it all in. The day had become blisteringly hot and the press of people almost claustrophobic as they entered the large square. This, Tory realized with surprise, was life—a far cry from the dull, safe existence she'd always led.

Vendors had set up their wares in stalls that displayed the brilliant colors of the Mediterranean. The sunshine bright yellow of lemons, the translucent green of the grapes and the glossy black of olives. Some of the stalls were piled high with fruits and vegetables, others groaned under the weight of fresh fish. Local women had set up their crafts between the produce booths and the small sidewalk cafés. She wanted to absorb and touch and feel it all.

Nobody just talked—they shouted. They yelled their opinions. They laughed. Hands and arms were used as punctuation, and Tory loved it. She felt alarmingly alive as she walked beside the man who held her life and that of her brother in his hands.

Marc was going to find Alex. Tory's heart pounded as she tightened her hand around his. She might never see Marc Savin again but she would remember this day forever.

Marc glanced down at her. "Okay?"

Tory nodded, melting against him as he pulled her close to avoid a run-in from a cluster of children playing with a puppy. She looked up at him when he didn't release her. "Is someone watching us again?"

"A couple of hundred someones." His voice was husky, and filled with amusement.

"You'd better kiss me, then."

"Yes. I think I had better do just that." He leaned against a wall and pressed his mouth to hers with a sweetness and tenderness that made her go limp.

"Do you think they've gone now?" she asked a little breathlessly as his head moved away and he looked down at her with a bemused expression.

He didn't even bother to look over her shoulder as he said huskily, "One more kiss should about do it." And bent back to his task.

They could have been alone on the planet, for all Tory knew, as she closed her eyes and leaned into him, feeling the warmth of his mouth on hers. When he eventually stopped they were both breathing hard. Marc took her hand as they moved back into the crowd.

They paused to watch an old woman with arthritic fingers make lace as delicate and intricate as a cobweb. If she hadn't been beside herself with worry over her brother, Tory would have loved to linger to buy some of the fine work, but Marc drew her away.

They had strolled several yards before Marc told her to wait, and he moved back through the crowd. Moments later he returned with a whisper-fine lace scarf, bought from the old woman.

Tory's eyes lit up as she took the creamy fabric from his hand. "Oh, Marc. Thank you. It's absolutely beautiful."

"Drape it over your arm," he said tightly. "It'll help hide the cast."

Hiding her hurt, Tory draped the lace over her right arm, hugging it against her body. What had she expected, for heaven's sake? That he'd bought her a present as a token of his esteem? She had to concentrate on what she was here for—to rescue her brother.

*Alex, where are you?* she thought desperately, again following closely behind Marc as he pushed through the crowd.

Silence was her only answer. She'd *know* if Alex was dead, she would have felt it. She was sure she would. Still, Tory knew they had to get to him soon.

Marc bought her a huge piece of coconut from a vendor and she ate it while they strolled away from the piazza and down one of the myriad side streets. Here the houses cast the narrow streets in deep shadow, making it marginally cooler. Tory finished the coconut and Marc waited as she went to a wall fountain to wash her hands.

He noticed how rigid her back was and cursed himself. He hadn't been able to resist buying that scrap of lace. Her eyes had shone for a moment when he'd given it to her. This was an op, not a vacation. The life of one of T-FLAC's best agents was hanging by a thread. If they didn't find Lynx soon, it might be too late.

Tory wiped her hand on her leggings and started walking toward him. She stopped in midstride, her head jerking up, the color draining from her face.

He took a step in her direction, then halted without touching her. "What is it?" Her eyes were glazed as she stared blankly over his head. He was about to shake her when he realized what was happening.

She'd found her brother.

She stood frozen in place. He was afraid to touch her lest he break the communication.

Marc swiftly scanned the narrow alley. Water splashed into the verdigris basin beside him, misting his arm with cool water. The noise of the hundreds of people crowding the piazza a few blocks away was muted, the street shadowy. Thank God there was no one in sight.

He ached to hold her, but his hands clenched into tight fists as she swayed slightly. He was in big trouble.

She was a major distraction at a time when he could least afford any mistakes.

Tory was a civilian. He'd had no intention of getting within ten feet of Victoria Jones. Unfortunately he'd miscalculated badly. If it had been pure lust, he could have dealt with it. Unfortunately, that wasn't the case.

Victoria brought out a tender side of him he'd never known. There was something about her that got under his skin; something that tugged at that secret place he'd buried and forgotten long ago.

He leaned back against the rough wall, keeping his eyes moving constantly to make sure she was safe. She was vulnerable, especially now with all her energies fixated on communicating with Alex.

He wished to God she'd snap out of her trance so he could get her safely back to the grotto. The angle of the sun reminded him that considerable, precious time had passed as they'd wandered through the market.

He reached out a steadying hand when he saw her jolt, as if waking from hypnosis. "Are you all right?"

She blindly gripped his fingers, and Marc pulled her against him, encircling her with his arms. Holding him just as tightly, she pressed her face against his shirt. He could feel the warmth of her tears soaking his shirt; but she cried silently, her body barely moving.

Tilting her face up with his finger, he scanned her still-pale skin. "You don't have time to fall apart. Do you hear me, Victoria? No time, princess." He hardened his heart as she looked up at him with eyes awash with fresh tears. "Give me the where and what, and you're on your way back to camp." She swallowed several times, dashing her fingertips across her cheek. "He's being held at the Palazzo Visconti." She stepped away from him to dip her hand into the fountain and splashed water on her face. "Only one man is guarding him now. But there are more than twenty upstairs in the palace." Her voice was flat and devoid of any emotion.

Marc's eyes narrowed. "Upstairs? Don't tell me—"

"I thought Alex said 'dungeon'—" Tory looked up at him. "Surely I must have misunderstood."

"'Fraid not, princess." Marc was grim. "The Palazzo was built in the early 1400s, complete with a moat and dungeons." He frowned. "Did you get anything else?"

Tory ran the random, fragmented dialogue through her mind to get it straight. "He says there is a secret door into the palace from the park—but there are motion detectors on all the other entrances. The public isn't allowed to visit the royal suites, and that's where Spider is." Tory grimaced. "I'm not even going to ask. Alex says he has a couple of broken ribs and the perfect nose you always ragged him about will never be the same. They change the guards irregularly, they do a lot of drinking after ten, and seem to be pretty lax."

She chewed her lip. "Marc, Alex said to tell you to be especially careful. Someone inside wants you badly enough to have set this whole thing up. Alex said they're waiting for you but...but you have no face. Does that make any sense?"

"It's what I was expecting," he replied, his tone grim. "Did Lynx tell you anything else?"

"He believes the bird can still fly." She frowned as Marc urged her back the way they had come, bending to pick up the scrap of lace that had slipped from her arm. "What 'bird'? A helicopter?"

"Yeah." Marc grinned. "The Hughes 500 chopper that Lynx flew in. We thought we'd lost it. The Huey... Damn, that's great! At least we have one piece of good news. It sure beats waiting around for Angelo. With the helicopter in commission we can fly out."

"Where are we going now?" Tory adjusted the lacy fabric over her cast and walked faster to keep up with his long strides.

She tried to read his expression, but his face was suddenly shuttered as he lost the smile and his jaw tightened. "I'll take you back to the truck. Your part in this is over."

"Oh, but…"

Marc turned and pinned her in place with a fierce look. "You go back to the grotto, no ifs, ands or buts about it. Got that?" His mouth was hard. She nodded. "Don't try and play the hero, Tory. There's no need. I'll get your brother out. By this time tomorrow, Marezzo will just be a memory."

She tried to pull her arm out of his grasp. "You're hurting me."

"Not as much as those sons of bitches will if they catch up with you again." He dropped his hand from her arm, surprising her as he flung his arm around her waist and pulled her close to his side. "Keep close, keep your mouth shut and walk."

She didn't have much choice. The square was still crowded and noisy, and the press of people and Marc's arm kept them as close together as conjoined twins. "I hate to bring this up, but I'm starving."

"I gave you coconut."

"I want real food." Tory glanced up at him as they had to pause to let one of the vendors, pulling a cart piled high with produce, go by.

As soon as their path was clear, Marc stopped and bought her a square of pizza. He waited while the vendor rolled it in paper and handed it to her.

"Are you sure you can find your way back?"

Victoria's mouth watered at the savory aroma of garlic and tomato. "Yes, I can find my way back." She saw the way he scanned each face in the crowd. "In fact, I can even find my way back to the truck on my own. Go ahead." She could feel his impatience as he tightened his hand around her waist. "It's not helping Alex if you have to waste time leading me about when I'm perfectly capable on my own."

They'd come to the wide gate and Tory turned to look up at him. "The truck's right over there, I'll be *fine*."

For a moment he looked as if he was going to say something, but Tory put her fingers against his lips. "I'm a big girl. Go. Be careful," she said softly, standing on her tiptoes to kiss his unsmiling mouth. Before he could respond, she turned and walked away.

She could feel his eyes boring into her back and knew the moment when he turned and walked behind the high walls of the city.

It was so hot, and her heart pounded as Tory hurried toward the battered vehicle. Marc would get Alex out. She knew that.

It wasn't until she eased between the ancient pickup and the wine truck that she saw the man. He was leaning against the passenger door of the wine truck, and she'd have to squeeze past him to open the driver's side door of the truck.

He was about her height but wiry, with bulging muscles and brown eyes that surveyed her up and down. Tory shivered despite the heat. He looked like trouble.

For an instant she considered going back around her vehicle and climbing in through the passenger door. The man took a drag on his cigarette and flicked it into the dirt at his feet. Smoke spiraled from his nose and his eyes narrowed as she paused indecisively.

Tory glanced over her shoulder as she heard the whisper of footsteps in the sand behind her. Another man stood there, barring her retreat.

She recognized the second man and a shudder rippled through her body. Giorgio had been one of the two men who had held her in Pescarna. The hot metal of the truck pressed into her shoulder blades. The man who had tossed down his cigarette moved toward her, and Giorgio effectively blocked her way from behind. The pizza she'd been holding dropped to the ground unnoticed. Tory glanced from one to the other. She desperately forced the air in and out of her lungs.

Think Victoria. Don't panic.

"*Buon giorno,* Signorina Jones." Giorgio moved between the trucks until he was just an arm's length away from her. "You have met Mario. Yes?" Tory recoiled from the smell of garlic on his breath and the stink of old sweat that permeated the still-hot air.

Of the two, Giorgio was a known quantity and therefore the most dangerous. She shot a glance at the other man, hoping she could evoke some sense of chivalry. She'd never seen such cold brown eyes. Okay, no help there.

She was trapped between the two vehicles and effectively cornered by her two assailants. For a moment she considered hurling herself into the bed of the truck. The sides were just too high and Giorgio and Mario were closing in.

Could she attack them if they came any closer? With what? She wished she had one of Marc's nasty-looking guns. A knife would have been good. She didn't even have a toothpick, for God's sake.

If only...

Her arm thumped against the wheel well. Wait a moment, she did have a weapon—of sorts. The heavy plaster cast.

The man on her left grinned showing large yellow teeth. "You come back for Giorgio, yes?"

Tory frantically glanced back and forth between the two men. The market was still crowded with people. Surely if she stalled these two long enough, someone would come out and help her.

Her shoulders ached from pressing against the truck. Her braid, still hooked under her shirt in back, made a lump that chafed at her skin. She could feel the sweat running down her sides and trickling down her face. The salt stung her eyes, but she was too terrified to blink.

."You come with Giorgio now."

Victoria shook her head. "No, thank you, I have to go. I'm meeting a friend and he'll be worried about me." She hated the way her voice shook. Still no one was coming to her aid. Somehow she was going to have to extricate herself from these men and get away.

With surprisingly steady legs she moved toward Mario. "It was interesting meeting you, but I really have to go now." Tory came abreast of him. She gave him a weak smile, her heart pumping as she moved past him, managing to grab the door handle.

Lord, I did it.

Yanking the handle down she pulled at the door. It stuck and she pulled harder. As the door flew open, she felt a hand grab her hair. Her scalp stung as Giorgio gripped the hair at the nape of her neck, his fingers tight, painfully snagging the loose hairs. Her eyes stung and the baseball cap fell unheeded to the ground.

"Signorina will come now." He pulled at the braid until it was free of her shirt, twisting it around his beefy wrist, jerking it so her head was tilted back painfully. Terror blurred her vision as Tory struggled against his grip.

"*Andiamo!*" Garlic breath seared her face as he spat the command. She had no idea what he'd said, but he was pulling her inexorably toward the back of the truck.

Tory kicked him; he merely laughed, calling to Mario in Italian as he dragged her backward. She managed to roll her head, sinking her teeth into Giorgio's wrist.

Snarling an oath, Giorgio tightened his grip on her hair. Tory didn't feel the pain. Her jaw ached as she held on for dear life while he talked furiously to Mario.

A steely arm slammed across her throat as Mario lifted her easily off her feet. She dangled helplessly between the two men.

Her jaw seemed locked, despite the arm across her

windpipe. Lights danced before her eyes as the arm across her throat pressed harder. She wanted to draw in a lungful of air, but she knew if she relaxed they would take her.

Giorgio fired a command in Italian at Mario, who immediately pinched her nose between foul-smelling fingers. Tory's jaw unclamped as she sucked in great drafts of burning air through her mouth.

The metallic taste of blood was on her tongue and she spat it out. Right on Giorgio's fancy handmade shoes. She hung limply in Mario's arms, his forearm still across her throat as she struggled to breathe.

Dizzy and faint, Tory forced her body to remain limp. She was beyond terrified. Death was preferable to what she knew Giorgio was capable of doing to her. Oh, God. She couldn't go through that again. She just couldn't.

Without warning she lashed out, both legs coming up and hitting Giorgio in the stomach, and he fell backward with a cry. Mario, who was still holding her, started backing up in surprise, pulling Tory with him as Giorgio staggered to his feet. She jerked out of his grip and swung her right arm up. Her cast hit Giorgio across the nose with a satisfying crunch. Pain shot up her arm. Blood spurted from the man's broken nose.

Turning toward Mario, she used her knee with all her strength and he crumbled, screaming, cupping his groin with both hands.

Leaping over his crouched body, Tory ran for the open door of the truck. Sliding across the seat she fumbled with the door latch with her cast and frantically searched under the seat for the key.

The door wouldn't lock. Straightening, she used her good hand to try to force down the little chrome button, her heart in her throat. She leaned over and slammed down the button on the passenger side, but the driver's side wouldn't lock, no matter how hard she tried.

She still couldn't locate the key. Peering through the grimy window, she saw Giorgio shaking his head, blood still spurting from his nose, as he lumbered between the vehicles toward her.

Where's the key? Where the hell is that key? Tory ran frantic fingers under the seat again and again. The key was gone. Sliding across the seat, she managed to unlock and fling open the passenger door. She catapulted out and took off at a dead run. They were between her and the safety of the crowds. She had no choice. There was an open field to her left. Beyond that a stand of trees that might offer some protection. If she could make it.

Not looking back, she sprinted for the field, her bangs stuck to her forehead, wet with sweat. Her arm throbbed painfully. Within seconds, the force of a body cannoning into her from behind took her down, and she gasped in a mouthful of powdery dirt as she hit the ground.

Giorgio's body pinned her as Tory twisted and kicked, screaming for help as she tried to escape from beneath the knee he'd pressed into her back.

She was lying facedown, the weight of his body holding her firmly as she bucked and squirmed uselessly. With a punishing grip, he flipped her over on her back, his face contorting murderously. The cast was handy for another swat. Unfortunately, this time it only connected with the side of his head. He roared his rage.

Fatalistically, Tory saw his elbow lift. She closed her eyes tightly as his fist connected on her jaw with brutal force.

*VICTORIA, OPEN YOUR EYES. Wake up. Now!*

*Alex?* Victoria's eyes fluttered but refused to open. *Alex, are you...are you all right?*

Forcing open her eyes, she glanced around as she rotated her jaw. It ached.

She could hear her brother's amusement in her mind. *Honey, I'm fine. Let's concentrate on you, okay? Where are you hurt? Can you move?*

*Where are we?*

*The bowels of the earth, at the "hotel" Palazzo Visconti.* His tone was rueful and bitter. *Tell me what you see.*

The room was about ten feet by ten feet. Stained blocks of stone formed the walls, floor and ceiling. The only furniture was the bed she was lying on—a bare dirty mattress that was cold and damp with mildew and other things she didn't want to identify.

There was a tiny window high in the wall above the bed that let in a little of dusk's meager light. It was certainly too high to reach and too small to crawl through even if she could. She stifled a groan.

*Tory?* Alex's voice was near, but she still had to close her eyes to concentrate because he sounded weak. *How badly are you hurt?*

She moved her jaw again, cautiously. It hurt, as well it should after the punch she'd taken from Giorgio's fist. Her broken arm throbbed under the cast. *No major problems.* There was absolutely no point in having Alex worry needlessly.

Tory heard a door open and close nearby. She squinted at the door to her cell. Constructed of heavy dark wood, raw and stained with hundreds of years of moisture, it was banded by wide metal strips. Very old but with a depressingly modern-looking locking device.

*Alex?*

She shifted restlessly on the narrow straw-filled cot. *Alex?*

There was no response.

She mentally called his name several times before she felt him inside her head again. *What happened?* she asked frantically.

*They're coming your way. They think I'm your boyfriend, but it's Marc they want. Do you hear me, Tory? They want Phantom…. Don't tell them.*

Tory heard loud noises coming from down the hall where she knew Alex was being held and heard the key grate in the lock on her door.

She was paralyzed with fear as three men came into the room, shutting the door behind them. "Good evening, Miss Jones."

She had only seen Christoph Ragno once when she was being held in Pescarna. The memory would live with her for the rest of her life. Tory swallowed the bile threatening to choke her. "Why was I brought here?" she demanded in a tone that reminded her of her grandmother. "I want to see the American consul. You have no right to hold an American citizen like this."

"You have no rights here, Miss Jones. I thought I had made that obvious the last time you visited Marezzo."

Tory forcibly pushed the memories aside, biting down hard on her lip to ground herself. Coward or not, she had to keep her head. Alex was close by and Marc was sure to figure out where they were. Eventually. All she had to do was keep as calm as possible and not incite this man to violence.

Ragno's head was too big for his body. His greasy hair could have been blond and clung thinly to his pink scalp, and he had ears like sugar-bowl handles. His face was florid and shiny. Tory couldn't control the tremor that raced up her spine as his light brown eyes seemed to touch her skin.

"You had no right to detain me last time and even less so, now. You know that I'm—"

"I believe you already know Giorgio and Mario?" His lips stretched into a gruesome smile over large teeth as he nodded toward the two men standing against the door.

Tory spared an unsympathetic glance at Giorgio's swollen nose. Mario shot her a murderous look.

"What are you doing back on Marezzo, Miss Jones? I thought you had enough of our hospitality the last time you visited?"

"I want to see the U.S. Consulate." Tory told him, striving to sound calm when her insides shook at the menace in his eyes.

"We have your lover, Miss Jones," Ragno announced in a sibilant voice that grated on her nerves.

Did they mean Marc or Alex? Not that it mattered, she wasn't in any position to ask without risking the lives of one or both.

"He also says that he arrived in Marezzo for a vacation." Ragno assessed her, his watery brown eyes sharp. "He, of course, has been enjoying our hospitality for several months, awaiting your arrival."

He was talking about *Alex*. She tilted her chin. "If some man said he's my lover, then he lied to you. I came here on my own. I arrived this morning from Naples."

She screamed as he grabbed her hair and wrenched her head up, exposing her throat. He held a small sharp razor against her cheek.

"Stop lying, *puttana*. There was no flight from Naples today."

She stared at his face, inches from hers as he twisted her hair in his fist, and tears smarted in her eyes. "I... I came on the mail boat." Oh, God, she prayed that the mail boat had arrived this morning. She was amazed at how easily the lies were popping out of her mouth.

She felt his hand relax slightly against her head, and she winced as he pulled her up close to his soft body. "I will check on that." Still gripping her hair in his fist, he jerked his head at Mario. The other man nodded and slipped from the room.

The razor came up against her cheek again, icy cold as he pressed it to her face. She felt cold sweat bathe her skin. "Where is Phantom, Miss Jones?"

Tory looked blankly at him. "Phantom? Who..."

Letting go of her hair, he slapped her. Hard. "Tell me where Phantom is. *Now.*" Spittle sprayed her face as he yelled. She flinched before his hand arced and he slapped her again, hauling her up as she slumped sideways.

Tory sobbed. "I don't know what you want. I don't know anyone called Phan—"

He hit her again, holding her head still as he wound the yard of hair in his fist.

Her head reeled and her face throbbed as she felt darkness closing in. Just before she passed out, he released her hair, grabbing the front of her T-shirt instead. Holding her still, he brought the razor down with a terrifying stroke that slashed the cloth from neck to hem.

# CHAPTER TEN

TORY STAGGERED BACKWARD as he held the sharp instrument up. "I'll give you one hour to regain your memory, Miss Jones. Then I'll let Giorgio pay you back for your little dance in the parking lot. Giorgio isn't as fond of the ladies as I am, are you, Gio? Or perhaps you'd prefer Mario? I know he would like to prove to you that he is still very much the man."

He shoved her—hard. She hit the bed, sinking into the filthy mattress and gasping for breath, her ears ringing from the blows.

In the dim recesses of her mind, she could hear Alex's voice calling her name. She pushed him away with her last scrap of strength. Her eyes locked on the pale shiny face of Ragno as he stood over her.

Tory's whole body shook as he leaned closer and trailed the razor down the bare skin exposed by the slashed shirt. "I enjoy playing as much as the next man, Miss Jones." Ragno's loathsome voice snaked across her skin as he leaned in, close to her face. "Obviously, Giorgio didn't warn you sufficiently on your last visit. I can assure you that I have absolutely no compunction about the methods I'll use to make you talk. I'll give you one hour to tell me where Phantom is."

Straightening, he jerked his head at Giorgio and the two men shut the door behind them. Tory heard the rasp of the key in the lock from the outside, and she cradled her hot cheek in her shaking hand.

She crouched on the bed, too weak to stand, staring unseeingly at the door. She shook so badly that she couldn't stay upright, and she allowed her body to roll back on the bed. Curling into a fetal position, she felt the tears course down her face as she sobbed uncontrollably.

*Victoria!*

Alex! She couldn't let him know. He'd go ballistic.

*Damn it, Victoria, answer me. Right now.*

She sat up, jamming her hand against her mouth to stop the jerky sobs she couldn't prevent. And she blocked her thoughts as hard as she could until she was calmer.

*I'm all right.* She managed, moments later. The lie held barely a tremor.

*What did those bastards do to you?*

*Ragno knows that Marc's here. Oh, God, Alex. He knows.*

*Calm down. He doesn't know anything. Do you hear me, Tory? He doesn't know squat. He was fishing and hoping, but he doesn't know about Marc.*

*They're coming back in an hour to get me…. Alex, I hate this.*

*I know you do, honey.* Alex's warm comforting voice came through loud and clear. *Did you tell Marc everything I told you?*

*Yes.*

Relief bathed his words as he said calmly, *Then he'll come for us. Get yourself together and try to calm down. Can you do that, Tory?*

*What's the alternative?*

*That's my girl.* Alex gave a rusty laugh. *Just hang in there.*

She was hanging in there an hour later when the door opened. In the pitch-dark room, she had to squint into the light from the hallway. Her heart sank to her toes when she saw the bulky outline of Giorgio.

The dim lighting couldn't conceal the malevolent gaze directed at her over the swollen flesh of his broken nose. "*Capo* wants you. Upstairs."

Clutching her ripped shirt between her trembling fingers, Tory gave him a wide berth as she went through the door.

She'd managed to close the two pieces of fabric over her bra and belt it tightly around her waist so that she was marginally covered. She shot him a dirty look when he leered at the exposed swell of her breasts as she passed him.

"Right," he instructed, walking behind her. Tory obediently turned right down the stone corridor. She felt Alex two doors away, and drew strength from his thoughts.

The air was stifling. Hot and humid and heavy to breathe as Tory stumbled ahead of her guard. The flashlight he held illuminated only a few feet in front of her and she stumbled on the uneven floor.

"Left," he directed.

She turned when Giorgio said, "Turn." Walked up steps on command and kept her stiff and sore back ramrod straight. She was sick to death of macho men. She hated scary, threatening men. Hell, she hated being scared period.

There was light ahead and Giorgio turned off his flashlight. "Walk." He pushed her ahead of him with the metal tube of the flashlight. Tory wanted to smash his broken nose a second time just for the satisfaction of hearing him scream again. She tilted her chin and kept her eyes fixed firmly ahead.

A ten-foot-high elaborately carved mahogany door stood closed before her. She moved aside and waited while he opened it with a key, then cautiously stepped into the room.

A magnificent Persian carpet, in shades of cream and burgundy, stretched over a dirty and aged white marble floor. As Giorgio marched her across the carpet, she could see several black heel marks scuffed into the light-colored fibers.

Overhead was a frescoed ceiling. On the walls hung priceless paintings. Their elaborate gilt frames, however, were adorned with cobwebs, and the delicate brushwork was muted by dust. A magnificent gilded table stood against one wall, where a three-foot-high Venetian glass vase held what must have been an artistic arrangement of cut flowers. Long-since dead, brittle and brown leaves and petals were in piles on a tabletop thick with dust. The whole place smelled musty.

Their footsteps were muffled by the thickness of the carpet as they passed white Carrera marble statues and other incredible objets d'art, all of which needed dusting. Tory held back a sneeze.

At the far end of the room, seated on enormous burgundy velvet couches, sat three men. One to each sofa.

Giorgio prodded her with the base of the flashlight again as her footsteps lagged. The closer she got, the more Tory's apprehension grew. Her heart lodged in her throat, and her nerves were raw.

She recognized Ragno, but the other two men had their backs to her.

"*Eccola*," Giorgio said nasally.

Ragno rose, his expression hidden from the men behind him. The pale hand he wrapped around Giorgio's upper arm trembled with fury. "*Grazie,* Giorgio," he said loudly, then continued in a furious undertone. "Your timing needs improving. Can't you see that we have unexpected company?" His sibilant voice sent a shiver up Tory's spine. She winced as Ragno's thick fingers dug into her bare arm.

His pink sausagelike fingers looked ridiculous holding a delicate crystal wineglass. He took a sip and looked at Giorgio over her shoulder. "Did she give you any trouble?"

"*Nessuno, signor.*"

"*Buono.* Wait outside until I call for you."

Tory heard Giorgio's muffled footsteps as he walked away.

The fingers on her upper arm tightened. "Watch what you say, Miss Jones. If our visitor suspects anything unusual, you will both die."

Out of the corner of her eye she saw one of the men cross his legs. She kept her eyes warily on Christoph Ragno. His scalp reflected the light from the gigantic chandelier overhead.

Grasping her arm in what could look like a solicitous gesture, he led her toward the three couches. Tory's skin crawled at his touch, and she tried to pull her arm away. His fingers squeezed her upper arm warningly.

She glanced down at the man seated on the sofa.

And almost fainted.

*Marc.*

His expression was politely blank as he inclined his head in greeting, but his pale eyes blazed with warning.

"Come and sit down, my dear Miss Jones, and let me introduce you to my companions."

Tory shrugged off Ragno's hand as he led her to a sofa. She sank down, and accepted a glass of wine. She was sure all three men could see the pulse throbbing in her throat. She dared not look at Marc, who sat across from her.

"This is Samuel Hoag." Tory turned a stiff neck and looked at the other man. He was tall and painfully thin, with black hair that was parted neatly on one side. A small mustache cut across his thin upper lip, giving him a sinister, movie-villain look. She righted her wineglass as it slipped on her knee. There was something repulsively hypnotic about him.

His eyes, behind rimless glasses, looked deceptively benign as he stared back at her without expression. He had enormous pale hands that stuck out of his jacket sleeves like a nightmarish character from a Tim Burton movie. Tory shivered, the stem of the glass pressed into her palm.

"And this is our new friend, Sir Ian Spenser."

Marc toasted her with his wineglass, his face bland. "Charmed to meet you. Miss Jones, is it?" His British accent was so plummy it belonged in a Christmas pudding.

Tory took a hasty sip of wine and choked back a response.

She had absolutely no idea where or how Marc had procured the fabulous suit he wore. It was expensive and Italian designed, in a lightweight fabric that flattered his long legs and hung beautifully from his broad shoulders. A slim gold watch was barely visible beneath the correct half inch of white Egyptian-cotton cuff. The finishing touch was a conservative old-school tie.

He looked absolutely, mouthwateringly wonderful. He also looked slightly bored as he sipped his wine and watched her as he would a stranger.

Tory didn't want to know what was going through Marc's mind as he looked at her bashed-up face and ripped T-shirt. She wondered just how Ragno was going to explain her odd appearance to "Sir Ian."

Ragno cleared his throat noisily in the silence. "Sir Ian will be our guest tonight. He came to see his old school friend, Prince Draven Visconti, who is vacationing in America this month with his family. Unfortunate that you missed each other, Sir Ian."

"Most unfortunate, old chap." Unfortunate indeed, considering that the prince had been assassinated several months ago. Marc rose to go to the bar. "May I?" His pant leg brushed Tory's ankle as he strolled by her. "More wine, Miss…Jones?" He held up the decanter, pouring his own before turning to the other two men when she mutely shook her head. She'd seen the nerve ticking in his jaw as he walked past her.

He was mad as fire, and Tory didn't have to be a mind reader to figure that out. The last person he was expecting to see here was her. Well, wasn't that just too bad! She certainly would have preferred being back at camp waiting, too!

Samuel Hoag sat stiffly in the corner of his sofa, his long legs stretched out. She fixed her eyes on the pale, hairless skin of his shin above his socks.

Hoag said, "No more wine," in a curiously mellifluous voice, while Ragno accepted, allowing Marc to refill his glass.

"Miss Jones was in a small accident at the marketplace this afternoon," Ragno said, smoothly accounting for her appearance. Savoring the wine, he shot Tory a warning look. "Mr. Hoag and I felt it best to offer her our hospitality in the absence of the royal family.

"I'm sure the princess has something suitable for you to wear for dinner, Miss Jones." He looked at her torn shirt with distaste. He called for Giorgio.

"Take Miss Jones to the family suite," he directed. "See that she is suitably dressed for dinner."

Tory managed not to look at Marc as she was removed from the room. But she could feel his gaze burning into her back.

When Giorgio opened the double doors, she noticed a man standing sentry outside—a blond version of Giorgio, with a gun holstered on his hip. The guard glanced curiously at her, and she edged her way past him, following Giorgio up a narrow circular stone stairway and along a dimly lit corridor.

The farther along they went, the more elaborate and elegant the furnishings became. They turned a corner and Giorgio gestured toward a gilt-and-ivory inlaid door.

"Princess's room." He took her arm, opened the door and roughly pushed her into the room.

She glanced over her shoulder as she shrugged his hand away. "How's your nose?" she asked with false sweetness.

He backed up, his fingers tenderly touching the grotesque swelling, and narrowed his eyes malevolently. "Signore Ragno said get dressed." He walked backward to the door, as if he had to watch her every movement. "Get dressed," he warned. "I'll come to get you."

"Don't hurry back on my account," Tory said to the closed door, as she heard the key turn in the lock.

She made mental contact with Alex to let him know what was going on, then did a quick inventory of the room.

It was quite beautiful, decorated in shades of lavender and purple with accents of white. Like the room downstairs, it was covered with a thick layer of dust, and the once-fresh flowers were dead and crumbling.

Tory caught a glimpse of herself in the full-length mirror and groaned. Her hair was a wild, tangled mess, her jaw sported the bruise from Giorgio's fist, and her cheeks were streaked with dirt and tears.

She headed for the opulent gold-and-white-marble bathroom. Filling the enormous tub would take up half her allotted time, but she didn't care. After sprinkling violet-scented crystals into the churning water, she went back into the bedroom to find something to wear.

When Giorgio opened the door a short time later, without knocking, Tory was ready. She'd washed and dried her hair and used the hot rollers she'd found on the dressing table. The princess's gigantic walk-in closet was filled with fabulous clothes for all occasions.

She'd wasted precious moments pulling out a few pieces of casual clothing, hiding them for a later escape. Then her fingers had lingered on several stunning evening dresses.

It was irrational, she knew, under the circumstances, but she wanted Marc to see her in something sophisticated, something…sexy. Marc, yes. The terrorists, absolutely not. She chose the most conservative gown she could. The princess hadn't had a modest bone in her body apparently. The dress Tory chose was probably for some formal state function. With apologies to the absent princess, Tory had managed to pour herself into the dress and pull up the short zipper at the back just as Giorgio walked in.

"Dinner's ready." He'd changed into an ill-fitting suit that was too tight for his lumpy body, and he stared at her unblinkingly out of swollen eyes.

"Lead on, Macduff," Tory said as she pulled on the shoes and picked up the sheer silk scarf she'd tossed on the bed earlier, draping it over her arm.

Giorgio gave her a blank look and gestured for her to precede him. They turned right instead of left this time and continued down an endless corridor, their footsteps muffled by the thick runner.

She caught a glimpse of herself in an enormous mirror at the top of the stairs. The heavily beaded emerald silk gown clung to her body as if it had been painted on. The low-cut, square neckline exposed more of her breasts than was wise, and she could feel her hair caressing her bare back. The billowing sleeves were caught at the wrist with elastic, effectively hiding most of her grimy cast. As she passed the mirror she realized with a sinking heart that while the dress had seemed deceptively modest in the bedroom, when she walked she exposed her leg to midthigh.

She stopped dead at the top of the wide staircase. She must be out of her mind. What had she been thinking about when she'd selected this particular gown? Marc, that's who.

The last thing she wanted to do was let those men see her like this. Tory quickly turned away from the staircase, almost coming nose to nose with Giorgio, who was right behind her.

He pulled his gun out from under his jacket and leveled it at her chest. *"Giú."*

"I have to change," Tory said firmly, swallowing her heart as he motioned her down the stairs with the deadly weapon.

*"Giú."*

"Look," Tory tried, tiredly. "I'll take two seconds to find something else and be right back." There was nothing less revealing. She'd *looked*. But perhaps she could pull something over the gown....

"*Giú. Down*." He pushed the gaping mouth of the pistol at the swell of her breasts, and Tory saw in his eyes how much he would love to pull the trigger.

He was the same height as she was in heels, and she was tempted to call his bluff, but one look at his dark eyes discouraged that idea. She sighed and took the first step down the red-carpeted stairs, holding on to the marble banister for balance.

Between the tightness and weight of the blasted dress and the unfamiliar high heels, she was liable to roll down the staircase and break her neck, so she made her way cautiously into the enormous foyer.

Giorgio grunted at a man standing outside the double doors. The guard swung the door open to the dining room, not bothering to hide the rifle resting over his arm. Tory shivered, tossing the ends of the sheer scarf over her shoulders so that it draped in front, effectively covering her cleavage.

The three men stood as Giorgio led her into the room. A painting the size of a small house adorned one wall. It was a breathtaking depiction of Palazzo Visconti before roads and modern civilization had blotted out the landscape.

The cherrywood dining table probably seated more than fifty people. The three men, still standing, were at the far end. Great. Tory drew in a deep breath, raised her chin and started walking.

"Miss Jones, how nice of you to join us." Christoph Ragno pulled out the chair beside him, and Tory gratefully sank into it, looking straight into Marc's eyes across the table.

For a moment she saw blazing heat before he picked up the fluted Baccarat glass beside his place setting and took a sip, his face bland.

"You found things to your satisfaction, I trust?" Tory hated the sibilance of Ragno's voice.

"Everything was quite satisfactory. No, thank you," she added, putting her hand over her glass as he held up the bottle of wine.

"You don't drink, Miss Jones?" Marc asked politely, accepting a refill. He looked devastatingly handsome in a black tuxedo and crisp white shirt. The diamond earring was back, flashing in his ear, and his hair was tied back. He looked exactly the way he sounded—sophisticated, wealthy, British and slightly bored. For a moment his pewter gaze rested hotly on her breasts filmed by the sheer silk.

She forced herself to respond lightly. "Not on an empty stomach, Sir Ian." She realized she was fidgeting with the silverware and dropped her hands into her lap, managing to shrug enough of her hair over her shoulder to cover more of her chest.

"Your face seems to be swollen, Miss Jones," Marc said mildly. "You must have taken a nasty spill this afternoon." If Tory hadn't jerked her head up to look at him, she would have missed the way his tanned fingers tightened on the stem of his glass and the way his lips thinned.

"Let's just say I came into contact with an immovable object." She could feel the heat of Ragno's

warning hand on her silk-clad knee. She twisted her
legs out of reach and took a sip of water, giving him a
furious glance over her glass.

God, would this never end? Beneath the thin veneer
of civilization at the table, the tension in the room could
have been cut with a knife. Ragno and Hoag had no idea
who Marc really was, she was sure of that. But by the
same token she could see that they were both wary of
him. Marc appeared mildly bored by the whole thing—
unless one caught a glimpse of his eyes, which were
simmering with rage every time he looked at her. What
was he going to do? How on earth was he going to
manage to get both her and Alex out right under the
noses of these men?

A white-uniformed waiter entered the room, and
Tory felt the rumble of her stomach. She was absolutely
starving, and she wondered how her body could still
function as if everything were normal.

The food was beautiful to look at and absolutely
inedible. The chef might be doing his job, but it was obviously under duress. While she tried to eat what tasted
like pure salt, she listened to Marc telling the other two
men of his friendship with the absent prince. He talked
easily of his business interests in England and Europe.
If she hadn't known better, she would have believed
every word. His impersonation was impeccable.

Far from filling the empty void in her stomach, the
food, either tasteless or so highly seasoned that she had
to gulp her water, had settled like a ball in the nervous
knot of her stomach.

The three men didn't seem to notice that she sat

silently without contributing to the conversation. Out-
wardly, everything seemed surrealistically normal.
Conversation flowed, wine was poured, courses served
and plates removed and replaced.

It was with enormous relief that Tory saw the last
dish taken away, and Ragno suggested coffee in the
drawing room.

Marc rounded the table and took her elbow as they
preceded the other two men out of the dining room.
Tory's heels clicked on the filthy marble floor, and she
was incredibly grateful for his support as they entered the
formal drawing room. Her legs felt like jelly, and her
heart had taken up permanent residence in her throat.
"What the hell induced you to wear— For God's sake,
keep your hair where it is, covering your chest." Marc
gritted under his breath as he led her to a white velvet ca-
melback sofa, his back to the other two. "And smile,
damn it."

Tory managed a credible smile, her heart in her eyes
as she arranged her hair so that it pooled in her lap, and
the long skirt so that it covered her knees.

Marc settled himself beside her, pinching the knees
of his pants and leaning back as if he didn't have a care
in the world. Tory felt perspiration beading her forehead
under her bangs.

The other two men took the sofa opposite and Ragno
indicated the tarnished, Georgian silver coffee service
on the table between them. "Will you pour, Miss
Jones?"

Tory shifted on the down-filled cushion, starting as
she felt Marc's hand on her hair. She shot him a startled

glance as he pushed her hair back from her face, but leaving long waves discreetly covering her chest.

"You have glorious hair, Miss Jones. I'd hate to see it trailing in the coffee." For a moment, as their eyes locked, they might have been the only two people in the room.

Marc felt the familiar heat when he touched her. It was an incredible risk that could blow his cover, but ever since she'd walked into the dining room, his fingers had itched to tangle in the glossy dark curls that flowed down her back and over the tantalizing swell of her breasts.

She avoided looking at him as she handed him his cup. Her face was pale, the swelling of her jaw an obscenity on her clear skin, despite the makeup.

Marc vowed he'd kill the bastard who'd hit her.

## CHAPTER ELEVEN

EVEN WITH HER EYES shadowed, Tory was incredibly beautiful in the figure-hugging green dress, her hair shiny and curling wildly down her back. How the hell had he ever thought her plain?

Marc let out a short frustrated breath and caught Samuel Hoag's assessing glance across the table. He shrugged as if to say, Yes, I find her attractive.

He knew he was playing a dangerous game. He had to get Lynx out. Tory's brother wouldn't be any help with his own rescue. Not with his injuries. But how much longer could Tory hold herself together without breaking? He couldn't carry them both out of here. Not at the same time.

Studying the two men, Marc mentally tallied everything he knew about them while keeping up his end of the conversation. Out of the corner of his eye he observed Tory wilting against the pillows. After several moments she blinked, then jerked upright and settled the cup back in its saucer, pushing her hair out of the way as she straightened her spine. He almost smiled as she tilted that combative little chin.

Besides the pain from the obvious beating she'd sustained, she must be both exhausted and terrified. They'd been up since the crack of dawn. She'd barely eaten anything at dinner and she'd been to hell and back today. She was holding up remarkably well, he thought, as he drank the strong coffee. He felt a surge of pride.

She'd gone along with his "Sir Ian" cover, but she was off balance and tired. Enough to blow the whole thing. He needed to get her out of the room.

Out of the palace. Off Marezzo.

Tory first, he decided. If he could get her out of the palace, and contact Angelo for pickup, he could sneak back inside and retrieve Lynx.

Yeah. Tory first.

Noticing the subtle tremor in her hands as she clutched the delicate cup, Marc said mildly, "It seems Miss Jones is about to fall asleep in her coffee." He rose and held out his hand to her. She blinked, her eyes glazed. "Allow me to escort you to your room, my dear."

Tory took hold of his strong fingers like a lifeline. "Thanks…I'd like to go upstairs now, I have a heada—"

"Giorgio will see her upstairs, Sir Ian. No need for you to bother yourself," Ragno interjected smoothly, snapping his fingers while pinning Marc with a warning look.

Marc helped Tory to her feet and waited until Giorgio came alongside her. He gave her a small smile and seated himself, watching the sway of her hips in the tight dress as the other man led her away. Her clean, shining hair caught the lights from the overhead chandeliers as it tumbled down her back.

"A beautiful woman," Marc said, leaning over to refill his cup as the door closed behind her.

Ragno glanced at Hoag and then back at Marc. "The attraction seems mutual, but not particularly wise."

"Do you think so, old chap? How intriguing." Marc raised one dark brow with amusement. "I think I'll have to go up and check on Miss Jones's…headache."

Ragno's eyes went cold. "I wouldn't be too confident of my welcome if I were you, Sir Ian. Despite the way she was dressed this evening, Miss Jones does not give the impression she is a woman who intends to share her sexual favors with a man she's just met." He glanced over at Hoag.

"We could perhaps procure a young lady from the village for Sir Ian, Samuel?"

Marc shot his cuffs as he rose, hiding his irritation with a cocky grin. "No need, old chap. Why send out for someone when I have what I want right here?" His smile widened as he murmured, "I think I'll just give it a go with my best shot. I say, are you a betting man, Ragno?"

TORY KICKED OFF her high heels as soon as Giorgio left. She was absolutely exhausted, but the coffee was coursing through her system, making her jittery and wired. She paced from one end of the opulent bedroom to the other before pulling at the zipper of her dress. As she was shrugging the heavy gown over her shoulders she heard a brisk knock at the door and her heartbeat sped up again. Surely not Giorgio? He would have just barged in. For a moment she paused, holding the dress securely against her thumping heart.

"Miss Jones?"

*Marc*. Tory stumbled to the door, tugging at the Queen Anne chair she'd wedged under the handle. She pulled open the door and almost fell into his arms.

She was about to say his name, but he put his finger over her mouth. "I found some aspirin in my room, Miss Jones. These should do the trick with that headache of yours. If you have a couple of glasses you can wash them down with this." He held up a bottle, and said under his breath, "Invite me in, damn it."

"That was very…kind of you. Please, come in." He still wore the tux, but had stripped off his bow tie and loosened the collar of the white shirt. A wedge of dark skin covered with crinkly hair showed through the opening.

He followed her into the room, closing the door behind him. Tory stood next to the bed, her hand still over her chest to hold up the weight of the loosened dress.

"I know you said that you weren't a drinker, my dear." He nodded his approval of the chair by the door. "But I think a couple of these and a glass of good Italian wine will fix you right up. You should sleep like a baby."

"That's very kind of you, Sir…Sir Ian. I'll get the glasses." Tory watched Marc prowl the room, and then turned to the bar and picked up a couple of crystal wineglasses. He'd removed his watch and was checking the room for…? What?

"Thanks." Marc took both glasses and set them on the bedside table. He lifted the shade from the lamp and nodded before pouring the wine. "Here you go." He handed her one of the glasses and made a noisy production of opening the pill bottle. "Two of these should get rid of that headache."

"Bugs," he mouthed, indicating the lamp with a jerk of his shoulder. Tory's eyes opened wide.

Bugs? As in someone listening to their every word? She looked at Marc with a small question and he nodded grimly. She motioned to her eyes. Can they *see* us? He shook his head, pointing to his ear. They could be seen, but not heard. "Keep talking," he said under his breath, as he continued to check the rest of the room. Every now and then she could see a little red light blink on and off. Another bug. She rubbed her arms trying to get rid of the chill.

She couldn't think of a thing to say as she stared at him blankly. He held up three fingers and came back to her. His hand slipped under the silky fall of her hair.

How could he think of sex now? Tory moved away but he grabbed her by the arm and drew her back, close enough so that she felt the heat of his body.

"You have beautiful hair, my dear. When I saw you at dinner tonight, all I could think of was having it wrapped around my body." His voice was husky, his eyes held a warning. "Say something encouraging."

She met his gaze, her mind totally blank. How could she hope to have two conversations at once, with his fingers stroking her neck? Tory closed her eyes and tilted her face. "Kiss me!" she demanded—to Marc and to their listening audience. She couldn't begin to come up with something that sounded even remotely subtle and seductive at the same time. Her mind was completely blank.

For a moment he paused and then with a muffled groan he took her offered mouth and kissed her hard. Tory wrapped her arms around his neck, straining to get closer as he used his lips and tongue to drive her out of her mind.

When he stepped away, the dress fell to the floor. Tory just stood there in her sheer panty hose and lacy bra as Marc moved swiftly about the room. Her breath was labored as he came back to her.

He stroked the swell of her breasts above the push-up bra and then shook his head. "You have a remarkable body, Miss Jones...Victoria, if I may? So soft, so smooth... Oh yes. Just like that. Is this an invitation, my dear?"

"Yes." Tory replied weakly as he pulled her over to the bed.

The springs creaked slightly as he pulled her down on the bed. A puff of dust settled, she bit her lip. The musty-smelling lavender satin spread felt cool on her heated skin. She started unbuttoning his shirt, desperate to feel his bare skin against hers. He held her hand away and shook his head.

"Let's get you out of this dress, shall we?" Goose bumps rose on her skin as he kissed her neck noisily. The dress was on the floor across the room, and she frowned. Of course. For a moment she'd forgotten that they were pretending.

"Where's Alex?" Marc whispered against her ear.

She closed her eyes and wrapped her arms around

his neck, pressing her face against his throat. "In the dungeon, directly below this room."

"Do that again, darling." He shifted so that the springs groaned, and used his teeth to nip at her neck until she moaned. Eyes triumphant, he whispered close to her ear, "Six stories down." His voice was grim. "Where's the belt?"

"The belt?"

Marc shook her so that the bedsprings creaked even harder. "The belt, Tory. The belt. Where is it? Concentrate, sweetheart. Would you like me to kiss you here?" he demanded in a normal tone. "What about here, love?"

"I can't concentrate when you do that," she whispered thickly.

He lifted his head slightly. "Your life depends on making this sound good."

She went cold as she remembered that two feet away, under the lampshade, was a listening device. Someone at the other end was hearing everything that went on in the room. She pushed her hair out of her face and nodded, her eyes dark. "Oh, yes. Kiss me there." Her voice shook with nervousness. "On the chair under the window," she mouthed to him.

Motioning that she continue moving on the bed, he got up silently and went to the window, rummaging under her clothes until he found the belt he'd insisted she wear that morning. It felt like months ago. Tory sat up and curled her legs under her panty-clad bottom. Every now and then she jumped up and down a little and tried to make sexy noises. She felt absolutely ridiculous.

Marc came back and slid across the bed. Tunneling his fingers through her hair, he whispered at the side of her face, "Can you communicate with Lynx and let him know what I'm doing?"

Tory nodded. The bedsprings rang out as he moved rapidly and let out a satisfied moan. Tory almost giggled hysterically, but he shot her a warning look. "Ahh…do that again. No. Harder, darling. That's it. Yes."

He moved cautiously to the end of the bed, lifting his leg onto the small upholstered bench at the foot. He raised his pant leg, and then motioned with his hand for her to keep moving.

Tory slithered around on the bed and made satisfied noises as he pulled a small eight-shot Sauer automatic pistol from his ankle holster.

"This damned bed is too soft," he said harshly. Pulling Tory off the mattress, he indicated the window.

"I don't mind the floor." Tory obediently followed him to the window.

"Tell Alex exactly what I'm doing." Marc pressed at a hidden device on the belt buckle and the backing opened. "God, woman, you're killing me." He checked the contents, pulling out a thin line, which he fixed to the buckle of the belt. Then he attached the gun to the line through the loop.

"Do you like this, darling?" Marc's husky voice was loud in the quiet room. Tory couldn't believe he could sound so aroused while performing totally unrelated tasks. It was hard enough for her just to concentrate on what to tell Alex. She scowled at him as he finished tying off the belt. "And this?" he said in a normal tone. "Answer me, sweetheart," he said very, very softly.

"Yes!" Tory hissed through clenched teeth. Marc opened the window quietly and started lowering the line down the outside wall.

"Tell Lynx to be watching his window. The belt and the Sauer are on their way down…. Lift your hips, darling. There, that's it. Does that feel good?"

Tory shivered as cool night air rushed in through the open window. "Y-yes." She tried to focus on what she was telling Alex. Marc gave her whispered instructions for Alex, while making lovemaking noises as he carefully lowered the belt.

She couldn't forget that someone was listening to every word. Tory wrapped her arms around her shivering body, and the moan she supplied was heartfelt and very real—the breeze billowing through the sheer drapes was icy on her bare skin.

"He's got it," she whispered, as Marc straightened, then drew the window shut. "He said he's as ready as he's ever been. He'll be waiting for you in two hours as instructed."

"Good," Marc whispered back. "Now, scream."

Tory looked blank. "Scream?" she mouthed, puzzled.

"As in climax."

Tory's face flamed. "They're *listening*."

Marc smiled and touched the side of her swollen jaw. "That's the general idea, princess. Scream your head off as if you are having the time of your life. Now."

Tory produced a mangled scream. Marc's credible

shout bounced off the walls. Still clutching her bare midriff, she shivered.

Marc pulled her half-naked body close and wrapped his arms around her. "Good girl."

He let her go and padded silently to the bedside table, picking up both glasses. He came back to her side and pressed a glass into her hand. Tory gulped down the wine until she felt its warmth stealing into her bloodstream. "Now what?"

"Now we take a shower." Marc's voice was thick as he took the glass out of her hand and set it on a nearby table.

"A sho-shower?"

She followed him into the bathroom and waited mutely as he closed the door, turned on the hard stream of water and started stripping off his clothes.

He unsnapped the front closure of her bra and tossed it on the floor. Her panties and stockings followed. Tory felt hypnotized as he tucked a hand towel around her cast and pushed her unresisting naked body under the warm spray.

"Now we can talk," he said with satisfaction as water sluiced down his face and over his broad shoulders.

The water plastered her hair against her skin as she stared blankly at Marc's hairy chest. How on earth could he switch on and off like this?

She gave a muffled, choked sob and tried to open the clear glass door. Marc pulled her back against his chest. Turning her in his arms he said huskily, "You were terrific, princess."

Tears filled her eyes and she bit her lip. "Petrified. I was absolutely petrified."

Marc's lips lowered to sip the water off her cheek. "This one is for us." His mouth slanted across hers and Tory choked back a sob as the sweet insistent pressure of his mouth opened hers.

The wet heat of his tongue and the familiar roughness of his chest sliding against her wet, naked breasts made her forget everything else. Desire flared in her, and her heart beat erratically as her nipples pressed against the familiar roughness and the hard muscles of his chest.

"Mmm." She couldn't get enough of him as she stood on tiptoe, her fingers clutched in his wet hair. His mouth ravished hers—too slowly, and she pressed her breasts flat against him, straining to get closer.

Her skin felt ultrasensitive as his hand traveled down her body, testing the shape of her nipples, the curve of her waist, the flare of her hips. He pressed her against the cool marble wall.

She slid her hand up the slick skin of his rib cage, tangling her fingers in the crisp damp hair on his chest. He smelled delicious and she darted her tongue out to taste him. She felt his nipple peak against the tip of her tongue and heard his groan of pleasure.

"The bed…?" she asked hopefully.

"We'd never make it." He nibbled at the tendons in her neck. "Besides—" he sucked her skin into his mouth, laving it with his tongue "—the first time we make love in a bed, it won't be with God-only-knows-who listening in." His breath fanned her neck deliciously. "Lord, I want you."

"You have me." Her body burned, yearning for his

until she was almost incoherent. She felt the compelling pressure of his large hands cupping her hips, pulling her more tightly against his erection.

Tory managed to hook one leg behind his, pressing him closer, to the aching juncture of her thighs, then rotating her hips until he moved his hands to grip her buttocks.

As he lifted her, pinning her against the wall, she wrapped her legs around his waist. With one thrust, he entered the willing, wet, warmth of her. Tory moaned low in her throat as his thrusts became more intense, the in-out movement of his hips sliding her between the cool marble wall and the blazing heat of his body.

She closed her eyes as the heat and pressure built. Marc rubbed his coarse black chest hairs against her nipples, drawing a tortured whimper from Tory. She tried to press her hips closer, but Marc slowed his thrusts until he was barely moving.

"Slowly, sweetheart, slowly. I want this to last."

Tory was beyond waiting. She used her heels to clutch his bottom and pulled with all her strength, undulating her hips until his body movements matched hers.

At last the unbearable waves of pleasure crested. With a cry, she climaxed. An instant later, he followed.

Water sluicing steadily against his back, Marc slowly lowered her to her feet and pushed soaking strands of her hair over her shoulder. His arm came around her waist as he soaped her and helped her rinse. Dizzy, she leaned her head against his chest while he washed himself.

Her knees felt weak, and her heart pounded, yet she couldn't meet his eyes as he helped her out of the shower and handed her a towel.

Steam filled the bathroom as the shower roared behind the closed glass door. Marc took the towel out of her hand and quickly rubbed her dry. He slipped his hand under her chin. "You okay?"

"Yes." But she knew she would never be okay again. Today had shown her just how very different they were. She would never in a million wishful years, be able to fit into his life. He certainly wouldn't fit into hers.

She was scared out of her mind, yet sexually aware of him all the time. A mere glance made her want him. She loved the touch of his hands and mouth. She loved the way he enjoyed playing with her hair. She loved the way his pale eyes ignited when he touched her.

She loved. And that was the problem.

Marc Savin was hazardous to her health.

"When can we leave?" Tory asked, keeping her voice low under the sound of the water and wrapping the towel around her body, and another around her head.

Marc ran his towel over his hair, using his hands to pull it back and tie it.

"I have to get Lynx out and to the chopper." He pulled on his pants and picked up his shirt off the floor. Ignoring the water marks on it, he shrugged it over his shoulders and started buttoning the studs. "Remember? I had you tell him I'd come down in two hours."

He took his watch out of his pocket, strapping it to his wrist. "That gives me about forty minutes to get you organized."

"I'm always organized," Tory said, sitting on the edge of the tub. "What do you want me to do?"

"I'm going to get you out first. Contact Angelo to pick you up, then come back for your brother."

"Alex has to be taken out first, Marc. You know that. If they keep torturing him I don't kn— I don't know how much longer he can hold on. *Please.* Please get Alex out first. I'll be fine until you come back and get me."

Marc pulled on his jacket and looked down at her. His face was savage as he cupped her bruised cheek with a gentle touch that made her chest ache. "I'm not fucking leaving you here alone. Right now you're nothing but a means to an end for them. What do you think they'll do to you when they decide you're no use to them?"

Scared out of her mind, Tory clutched his arm. "I'll come with you. I'll help you with Alex…"

"Tory—" his voice was gentle "—you told me yourself that he's badly hurt. I can't watch out for both of you. I'll end up getting us all killed. You can go back to the grotto and wait f—"

"I'll stick to you like glue," she begged. "I'll do everything you tell me to do. I swear. You can give me a gun…"

"Tory," Marc said reasonably. "I'm going to have to haul Alex out of here on my back, you know that. It's going to take everything I have to carry him *and* keep the two of us from getting our asses blown to hell. I can't watch *your* back at the same time. I'm not Superman, sweetheart."

*Yes, you are.* "Then take Alex first."

"This isn't up for debate. I don't have time to argue. Let's go."

As much as she wanted to run like hell, she couldn't do it. She'd come all this way to save her brother. "Alex first," she told him, keeping the tremor out of her voice with supreme effort. Bile rose in the back of her throat. "*Go*. The quicker you leave, the quicker you'll be back to get me out of here. They think we've just had wild sex and we're sleeping. Nobody is going to come in here until morning."

She *prayed* nobody came into her room until after she and Marc left.

"I'll be back to get you as soon as Lynx is secure." He rubbed his jaw. "If there was any other way, I'd take it. I hate like hell to leave you with those animals for even five minutes," he said, his voice grim.

She'd have to make do with that. She knew that it was the sensible, practical thing. But she was terrified what could happen to her being here alone.

## CHAPTER TWELVE

TORY WOKE to early-morning sunlight streaming through the window. The wet towel lay beside her on the bed, and her hair, still damp, was tangled around her. After Marc had left she'd tried to sit up against the headboard to wait. She hadn't meant to fall asleep, but the dark room, coupled with the exhaustion and stress of yesterday, had taken their toll.

Alex was gone. Thank God. He'd let her know he was safe. The relief she felt was like a physical lightening of her body and spirit. Tory didn't doubt for an instant that soon Marc would be on his way back for her.

She'd be ready.

The princess hadn't owned a pair of jeans, at least that Tory could find, so she'd pulled on a pair of beautifully cut black linen slacks and a white man–style shirt last night after Marc had gone. A pair of leather flats had been kicked off beside the bed last night, and she quickly slipped them back on.

She almost jumped a foot when the door opened and she spun around to see the malevolent gaze of Mario. He was carrying a cloth-covered tray.

"Breakfast? Good, I'm starving." The very thought of food made her sick to her stomach, but she knew she should appear as normal as possible. She thought she was fine until she saw who was standing behind Mario. Oh, God.

Ragno stepped aside and ushered Samuel Hoag into the room. With a single look from Ragno, Mario set down the tray, left the room and presumably went to wait outside. "You've been a naughty girl, Miss Jones." Ragno's malicious voice would live forever in her nightmares.

Tory felt bone-deep cold and the small hairs on her arms prickled as he moved closer. He was wearing an overpoweringly sweet and cloying aftershave that made her stomach heave. She swallowed down bile. *Marc? Hurry.*

"What do you mean?" *Stay calm,* she told herself. *Just stay calm. Marc will come—*

"I mentioned your little tryst with Sir Ian to my other guest last night." Ragno shook his head, his pink scalp shiny under his hair. "He was not pleased."

Tory raised her eyebrows. She wasn't quite sure which "other" guest he was referring to. The other man with him, or Alex? She lifted a go-to-hell brow as she'd seen Marc do. "Really?"

Ragno's sausagelike fingers tightened on the silver-headed cane he held in his right hand. "In fact he was quite furious." Ragno circled the room, picking up a dusty perfume atomizer off the dressing table, lifting it to his nose and then putting it down.

The footboard stopped her backward movement.

They were trying to play Alex and Marc against one another, thinking they were both her lovers. Tory hadn't a clue why they would care. But since it was clearly an issue, she was afraid to blink in case she missed something.

She glanced from Ragno, near the dressing table, back to Hoag at the door. "That doesn't surprise me, he's rather...possessive."

"Where is he, Miss Jones?" Ragno moved closer. She cringed inwardly as he stroked the icy metal head of the cane down her cheek.

Her heartbeat was manic, her eyes dry as she stared up into the man's empty gaze. "Where is who?"

The silver knob pressed against her cheekbone—hard. "Your former lover."

This time she knew he meant Alex. "I have absolutely no idea. He probably didn't like your hospitality any more than I have." The moment the angry words were out of her mouth, Tory knew she'd made a very bad mistake.

Cristoph Ragno tapped the cane harder against her cheekbone. It brought tears to her eyes. She bit the inside of her cheek, edging sideways.

Grabbing the hair tied at her nape, he said in a deadly voice, "We have two guards dead and another three wishing they were." He forced her head back and stared coldly into her terrified eyes. "Now, where are they, Miss Jones?" Samuel Hoag had moved from the door and closer to the bed to block her retreat. She tried to pull Ragno's fingers from her hair. "I...I d-don't know."

Sweat glistened in the pink lines around Ragno's

mouth. "We know both men are agents, Miss Jones. Not just any agents, but T-FLAC, to be precise. They have been messing in our business for years now. Poking their noses into things that are no concern of the United States. I am going to put a bloody end to that organization one way or another."

His fingers clenched her hair close to her scalp in a stinging grip. "I'll start by cutting off T-FLAC's head. It's taken us five years to catch even one agent. The man we've held all these months couldn't be broken. We still don't know his real name. If you hadn't arrived those weeks ago we'd have had to kill him. But we knew you'd be even better bait, Miss Jones. We had no idea just what your connection was, but Samuel was sure you would net us some results if we let you go and allowed you to run whimpering back to the States. And Samuel was, as always, quite correct."

*Oh no,* she thought. *My fault.*

"All you have to do is tell us which one is the Phantom."

Her mouth went dry.

"Now, you can do this the easy way—" he twisted a hank of her hair around his wrist and gave an excruciating tug "—or the hard way. I can assure you that either way will be satisfactory to me. Now I must admit that I'm the more—how shall I put this?—I'm the more physical of the two of us. But I can assure you that you will not enjoy Samuel's methods any more than you do mine. You are wearing my patience thin, Miss Jones. Consider this your last opportunity to speak."

That was what she was afraid of. Tory licked dry lips. "I have no idea w-what you're talking a-about. I don't know anything about spies, for goodness' sake… I swear, I don't know what you're talking about."

She was paralyzed with terror as she realized that, unless Marc was hiding behind that closed door right now, she was on her own. Falling apart and crumpling into a whimpering little ball was not going to save her. To hell with it. Either way, she was going to have to get herself out of this mess.

"If you don't let go of my hair right this minute I'm going to scream this pile of stone down and every government agent from every country on this planet will come and annihilate you! There are at least a dozen people who know exactly where I am and who I'm with. Now let me go!"

She screamed as he twisted her arm behind her back. He forced her arm higher, and the pain was exquisite.

Tory lashed out instinctively with her cast. The sound of it connecting with his face was blocked out by her own shriek of agony as he twisted her hand impossibly higher against her back. A thin trickle of blood oozed from his nose where her cast had connected.

Oh, God. So much for taking initiative.

"She must like pain," Ragno said mildly, taking out a crumpled handkerchief and dabbing at his nostril.

Ragno dropped her arm as suddenly as he'd grabbed it. It hung numbly at her side.

"I ask you one more time, Miss Jones. Where are they? And which one is the Phantom?"

Tory suspected they would give her only so much time to answer before they killed her. She was also pretty sure it wouldn't be quick or pleasant. "You keep asking me the same questions," she said, striving to sound reasonable. "The last time I saw S-Sir Ian was after dinner last night. He left me and I don't know where he went."

His arm lashed out and the cane whistled as it came down across her back. Tory screamed.

She saw the arm swing back again. It was stopped in midflight by Samuel Hoag's bony hand.

"I think Miss Jones has had enough, my friend. There are other ways…." Hoag said grimly, looking at her. "Aren't there, my dear?"

Tory gauged the distance to the door. With almost superhuman strength, she broke free from the two men and ran for the door. The handle slipped out of her sweaty grasp as she felt a hand on the back of her shirt and she was yanked off balance.

"No!" Using her legs, she kicked out at Hoag as he plucked her away from the door and dragged her back into the center of the room. He spun her around, and shoving her hard in the chest, he pushed her down on the bed.

Before she could even bounce, she was scrambling backward, stopping only when she was against the ornate satin headboard. "Don't come near me."

She could tell by the murderous rage in Ragno's face that it was a pathetic command. Hoag held him back as he tried to beat her with the silver-headed cane. The sound of the cane thumping the satin spread filled the room. Dust hung in the sunlit air. Tory stared at the glinting silver head as it came closer and closer. Her mouth dry, she pressed her spine into the soft fabric at her back, twisting her legs out of reach. It was a total waste of time, of course.

*Marc.* She pleaded silently, frantically, as Hoag opened the door and spoke to Mario in rapid-fire Italian, then slammed it shut, spewing even more dust into the air. Hoag jerked his head for Ragno to get out of the way and seated himself at the foot of the bed. Tory, now on her knees, scooted farther back, trying to make herself a smaller target.

"My friend is a little zealous in his quest for the truth, Miss Jones." His voice was deep and devoid of expression. Tory tried to stop shaking, and she fixed her gaze on his face.

Behind him, Ragno impatiently tapped the cane on the carpet. Its thumping sounds syncopated with the thump of her heart. "There are ways to make even a whore like you talk, and I assure you we will use every one of them until you do." He turned his head as Mario came back into the room, followed by Giorgio. Hoag motioned to the two men. "Hold her."

Almost catatonic with fear, Tory glanced from one side of the bed to the other. She had no idea what they were planning, but she knew it would be bad. Very bad.

She bucked and kicked with all her strength, but they managed to catch her flailing arms and legs and flattened her against the bed, spread-eagled.

Hoag lifted the small box Mario had brought in on the tray, extracting a hypodermic needle. Tory stared with morbid fascination as he plunged the end and a thin stream of liquid spurted from the sharp tip.

Her back arched off the bed as he came toward her.

The needle sparkled in the golden sunlight coming through the window.

She licked her parched lips. "Please. Oh please don't…" Her eyes went wild as he pushed up the sleeve of her shirt.

"A little phenobarbital, Miss Jones. It won't hurt a bit." She felt the first sharp prick of the needle under her skin then a stinging heat surged through her veins. Her vision clouded and her lids closed. Just before everything went black she heard Ragno say, "You gave her too much, goddamn it, Samuel. You gave her too—"

MARC FELT FOR THE PULSE at the base of her throat with fingers he had to will to remain steady. It was pitch-dark, but he hadn't dared turn on the flashlight. Her pulse was thready but stable.

"Thank God." He shook her by the shoulders, and she moaned. "Tory. Sweetheart." Urgency made his voice as cutting as a knife. "Wake up."

She didn't move. He shook her again. Harder this time, beginning to realize this was no ordinary sleep. They had ten minutes—fifteen, tops—before the dirtbags discovered the unconscious guards down the hall.

He pulled her upper body against his chest, her head flopped to his shoulder. Thank God they'd brought her down to the dungeon. He'd managed to find her after an hour of searching upstairs and then only with the unwilling cooperation of one of Ragno's men. But this location sure as hell beat hauling her from one end of the immense castle to the other to get out.

From here, it was a fairly straight route—up the back stairs and into the front hall. He wanted like hell to hold her and he needed to see her in the light to assure himself she was all right. He had time for neither.

"Damn it, Victoria, do you hear me?" he demanded fiercely, pushing her head off his shoulder and holding it in both hands. "If you don't wake up and move your ass, we're in some serious shit."

She moaned again, stirring in his arms. Her head moved to the side slowly, and she whimpered, trying to pull away.

"Marc?" Her voice was weak, but at least she was conscious.

He hauled her to her feet and waited a second while she got her balance. "Up and at 'em, sweetheart." She wilted against him. Marc forced her to walk from one side of the small cell to the other and then back again, keeping his ears tuned to any noises outside.

By the time he'd walked her back and forth a dozen times, her gait was steadier.

"Do you know what they gave you?" he asked urgently as he eased his supporting arm away to see if she was capable of standing on her own.

"Pheno…"

"Barbital."

She faltered, but Marc kept his hands off her. He was prepared and willing to carry her, but if she could stand on her own two feet all the better. "Keep walking. How long ago did they give it to you?" His voice was harsh in the darkness.

"This morning sometime. How long ago was that?"

"Too long," Marc said grimly. "The good news is that it should be pretty much out of your system by now. Keep walking," he barked, as her steps lagged. He heard the shuffle of her feet on the stone as he went back to the cot and tossed a canvas bag on the mattress.

"Ever used a gun?"

"No."

"Well, you're in luck. Time to learn a new skill. Come over here."

When she got close enough, he took her hand and wrapped it around the laser-sighted automatic. He tightened his fingers over hers when she tried to jerk her hand away. "Listen and listen good, princess. Both our lives depend on you getting yourself pulled together. Now, concentrate while I tell you how to use this."

After he was sure she understood the basics, he pulled her behind him and checked the corridor. Everything was quiet.

Keeping Tory at his back, Marc walked carefully toward the stairs. If anyone came now, they would be in one hell of a bind. There was nowhere to go. The wall sconces, spaced every twenty feet, cast dim amber light the length of the corridor. While the numerous shadows and recessed doorways could hide them, they could just as easily hide the tango's men, too.

He glanced at Tory out of the corner of his eye. Her face was stark white, and her eyes dark and terrified, but she was on her feet and moving. The automatic hung from her hand—away from her body as if she felt the damn thing would bite.

He used his own weapon to tilt the infrared up. "Keep it there," he said harshly. She nodded, gripping the gun more firmly between both hands. The damned cast interfered with the grip, but at least it looked as if it was at a usable angle.

The stairs ahead were curved and dangerous, and he motioned for her to stay directly behind him as he climbed steadily. If anybody decided to come down, they would be at a distinct disadvantage.

He breathed a sigh of relief when he saw the light at the top.

Still moving silently, he motioned for her to follow him as he kept to the wall, heading for the sitting room where he'd first seen her last night.

Finally reaching the double doors, he opened one and motioned her in behind him, then closed it silently. The room was empty and quiet as he moved to the door at the other end.

He cursed. The palace was enormous, with doors everywhere and a million places to hide. Unfortunately that meant there were hiding places for the bad guys, too. The only way out was through the main foyer and out the front door—if they were lucky enough to pass through undetected. He'd disabled the motion detector when he'd come in for Lynx, but that didn't mean that there wasn't some conscientious guard out there.

He thought of Lynx in the chopper, waiting for them like a sitting duck. How the son of a bitch thought he could fly in the condition he was in was beyond him. But he wasn't leaving without his sister.

Marc could understand the sentiment.

He glanced over his shoulder at her. The silk Paisley scarf tying back her hair had slipped, loosening the long strands, and her eyes were wide with fright. His gut tightened at the smudged tearstains on her pale cheeks. When she moved the barrel of the gun up a notch and tilted her chin, he almost smiled.

Bowed but not beaten. Damn, what a woman.

Admiration swelled his chest. He brushed the red mark on her cheek with a gentle finger while in his heart murder glowed like a fiery ember. He was going to enjoy killing these bastards. Enjoy every fucking minute of it.

"Let's go."

It was one in the morning, the household was asleep and the foyer was blessedly empty. He heard the scuff of her shoes behind him on the slick marble as his eyes scanned the wide-open expanse. The heavy front doors were about forty yards ahead of them. Beyond that was the drawbridge, then the formal gardens and finally freedom.

Marc dipped his head close to her ear and whispered that they were going to take a chance on cutting a diagonal across to the door. It was a calculated risk, made even more of a challenge when the scent of her hair distracted him for a millisecond. Keeping to the walls would give them more cover but would also take longer, and time was of the essence.

Ready to run, she mouthed. Her magnificent hair trailed down her back, one sleeve of her white shirt was still pushed up, and Marc could see the bruise made by the needle. A red haze of fury threatened to blind him.

Oh, yeah. He was going to enjoy like hell coming back to take care of those bastards. But first things first.

Gritting his teeth, he scanned the foyer one last time. Grabbing Tory's elbow, he sprinted across the slippery marble tile. He felt her skid and paused briefly to steady her, then dragged her close behind him again. Heat emanated from her body as she pressed close.

They reached the door and he quickly slipped its bolts. They groaned and rattled, but the door opened. After a quick reconnoiter he went through first.

In front of them was an immense courtyard. Marc held her back with his arm as he scanned the shadowy open ground between them and the gate in the far wall.

In the center was an enormous three-tiered fountain. There was no water spouting from it, and the moonlight glistened off the green moss and slime in the basins. The cover of running water would have helped silence their progress, but that was not to be.

High walls surrounded them on three sides; the dark windows of the castle were at their backs. The walls made good, deep shadows and he took her arm, pulling her past the shrubbery along the side of the castle, keeping in shadow.

She followed him closely, stopping when he stopped, keeping the same distance between them. He breathed easier when they had traversed the unprotected space between the castle and the surrounding wall. His feet flattened the tall weeds, making a path through the overgrown garden beside the wall. They were almost there.

He dared not take the chance that Ragno had snipers

positioned in the windows. Tory followed him, silent except for her ragged breathing.

Her face was deathly pale and streaked with dirt, with strands of hair plastered to her sweat-dampened skin. Marc cursed silently and nodded toward the pedestrian gate beside the tall portcullis that led outside.

She lifted the gun in her hands higher. They came to the small door in the wall that he'd left unlocked when he'd come in. "Almost there," he said under his breath, pushing it open and pulling her through behind him. It was too good to be true. Were Spider's men all so incompetent they hadn't noticed that she was missing? Marc glanced at his watch in the moonlight, surprised that it had taken them only sixteen minutes to get from the dungeon to outside the walls.

The medieval drawbridge spanned the moat, which was more fetid mud than water. Urging her to move faster, he sped across the warped wood timbers and toward the gardens and the cover of the trees.

He could smell the rotten stink of stagnant water, his feet biting into the gravel of the driveway. They would be clear targets, out here in the open. But there was no alternative; they had to make a run for it.

He stopped for a moment to look over his shoulder. "Tory, listen to me. We have to run hard for those trees over there. If you hear anything—anything at all— ignore it and run faster. I'll be right behind you."

"Okay." In the moonlight, her eyes were wide terrified pools.

Marc looked at the heavy gun clutched in her arms. He considered losing it so that she could run faster. But the fact was, whether she really had to use it or not, if something happened to him, she would at least have a chance of protecting herself. He pushed the laser-sighted gun more firmly into her grasp. "Remember how to use it?"

She nodded, "Red light, shoot."

"Let's go."

The moon, unfortunately, was almost full and it was as bright as daylight. Her white shirt was a perfect target as they ran hell-for-leather toward the trees, the crunch of the small stones under their feet sounding dangerously loud. As soon as they were under cover he would give her his shirt. But first they had to get there.

The gravel driveway circling the moat was a wide, pale, unprotected swath they had to cross before they could even get to the shrub-studded lawn and the small forest rimming the estate.

Their feet hit grass as they sprinted for the thick cover of the trees. A high-pitched whine warned Marc a second too late that their luck had run out. The force of the bullet grazing his forehead dropped him to one knee. The pain would come later. He ignored it.

Staggering to his feet, he felt the warmth of blood running into his eyes. Tory stopped dead, her white shirt blinding in the moonlight as she turned.

*No.* Black speckles obscured his vision. *No.* "Run like h—"

## CHAPTER THIRTEEN

GRAVEL CRUNCHED beneath the running feet behind them. Jesus. The bad guys were hot on their trail and closing. There was another ping as a bullet whizzed by and tore up the grass between them. "Get the hell out of here!" he yelled, as the air near his head parted from another bullet.

He swiped his bloody face with his forearm to clear his vision. It partially worked. Glancing over his shoulder he saw a muzzle flash, seconds later a barrage of fire came from the drawbridge. Somehow he managed to gather Tory under one arm, half dragging, half carrying her, twisting to spray the area behind them with a violent burst from his Uzi.

A black silhouette tumbled over the drawbridge. The muffled splash of a body hitting the muddy water was drowned out as another round of bullets ricocheted close to their feet. Grass and dirt sprayed as Marc pushed Tory forward, his arm propelling her as he returned fire.

"Go, for Christ's sake." He hauled her up as she stumbled in the soft dirt, and pushed her hard.

"I'm not leaving without you."

The fool woman turned back and waited for him as Marc staggered toward her, blood dripping into his eye. He caught at her cast and hauled her as fast as he could go.

A hundred yards.

Eighty yards.

Fifty yards.

*"Go. Go. Go."*

The once-manicured lawn took a beating, sod flying as bullets whizzed too close for comfort. He almost tripped over a boxwood hedge but kept pushing and pulling at Tory to keep her abreast.

The trees swayed slightly in the breeze, dark branches beckoning when he felt a sting in his leg. Then, twenty yards from cover, his leg folded under him and he fell to the ground.

Damn. The sons of bitches were in front as well as behind them. Surrounded, outgunned and outmaneuvered he struggled to his elbows, pointed the Uzi at a burst of light and fired off several rounds. There was a scream and a thud as someone bit the dust.

The Uzi was good for another sixty-four rounds times three, with the second magazine welded to the first, but at the rate the bad guys were coming, he would be out of ammo long before they were.

Again he sprayed covering fire into the trees ahead of him. It bought Tory precious seconds as the shooting stopped for a moment.

Staggering to his feet, Marc was in motion, aiming his weapon in an arc while in a lurching run. He had to get her out of range and the hell away.

All he could see of Tory up ahead was that damned white shirt through the branches. As he ran he tugged his black T-shirt over his head. The night air felt good as it cooled the sweat on his body. He couldn't feel the wound in his leg, but if he was capable of putting weight on it, it wasn't broken. That's all he cared about right now. Being mobile.

He pulled her down behind the cover of the shrubs. The heavy scent of gardenias permeated the air as he handed her his damp T-shirt. He blinked away the graying of his vision, doing a quick visional scan to be sure she hadn't been hit. "Put it on, and do it fast."

His breath was a choppy whisper. He could hear the goons thrashing about in the trees a hundred feet away. Not nearly far enough. It was mercifully dark, the tall trees and thick ornamental shrubs hiding them. But for how long?

Tory pulled his T-shirt over her head, then gave him a horrified once-over. "You're hurt!" Her cool hand moved over his face, as if she could fix him with her fingertips. "Oh, God, Marc. You're bleeding."

"Yeah, bullet wounds have a tendency to do that." He dug in his pocket and then grabbed her wrist as she tried to use the hem of the shirt to stanch the flow. "Here. It's the ignition key to a Vespa parked off the main road up there. Go."

With a jerk of his head he indicated the direction through the trees. "The moped is behind the barn. Drive it to where I picked you up in the truck, and get yourself to the grotto. There's no way we can get to the helicopter now. Alex is waiting for my signal. He'll pick you up."

"I'm not leaving without you."

"You'll damn well do as I tell you! Move your butt

out of here. Now!" The crashing of small branches drowned out his whispered words as men ran within feet of their hiding place. Marc put his hand over her mouth as she started to protest.

But she shook her head, her eyes huge over his hand. She wasn't leaving without him.

When the noise moved away, he dropped his hand and said furiously, "You're no goddamned hero. You'll get me killed if you stick around."

She flinched, but she answered flatly, "Then we go together. I'm not leaving. Warm up to the idea."

Marc thought quickly and put a sneer in his voice. "Just because I screwed you doesn't give you the right to hang around like a frigging leech. Have some pride, Victoria. I only wanted your body, not a lifetime commitment."

He heard the sharp hiss of her breath and pushed harder. "At least Krista was trained. She would have been some help."

He wished she wouldn't look at him like that and squinted off into the trees. "When I want a woman, it sure as hell wouldn't be some mousy little bookkeeper from the sticks." He looked her straight in the eye. "Get lost, lady. Your brother's waiting for you and I have things to do."

Ignoring the way her eyes narrowed and her chin tilted, Marc moved away from her, crawling deeper into the trees without a backward glance. Laying a track of firepower as he started to run, he was misdirecting their attention to himself. Away from Tory.

In moments he was swallowed by the dense underbrush. He continued as fast as his leg allowed until he was sure he was far enough away from her. He leaned back, using a tree trunk to rest his leg for a moment, hoping to God she could figure out where the hell the Vespa was.

He knew the only way to draw their fire was for them to follow him. Find *him.* Firing in the general direction of the palace, he crashed through the undergrowth, making enough noise for a deaf man to follow. He didn't have long to wait.

Mario came around a tree trunk, his eyes darting from side to side, an AK-47 assault rifle cradled in his arms like a baby. Marc took advantage of the man's surprise at seeing him just standing there in the glade.

Swinging his leg up in an arc, the side of his boot hit the rifle, sending it somersaulting into the bushes.

Mario's hands were now free, and he managed to get a glancing blow to Marc's face. He sidestepped, bringing the butt of his Uzi up and ramming it against the other man's cheek. Mario screamed in pain, his eyes feral as he swung again.

The blow landed on Marc's forehead, exactly where the bullet had creased him. Damn. Marc exploded, blocking the other man's blows and striking out in a flurry—left elbow to the throat, right fist to the gut. He swung his leg again, but the bullet wound made his arc too low and he hit Mario's shoulder this time.

Mario staggered back, blood pouring from his nose. He looked around frantically for help. There was none. Marc gave him a shove with the butt of the Uzi.

"How do you like feeling helpless, you useless piece of shit?" Marc punched him in the solar plexus. "This is for touching Tory." He swung again, knocking the other man's head to the side.

Finally he dropped Mario with a vicious uppercut to his jaw. The sound of bone crunching was extremely satisfying. Mario lay still, and Marc used the back of his free hand to wipe the blood out of his eyes. He was starting to feel a whole lot better. His adrenaline was pumping, he didn't even notice the blood on his face, and his leg was numb. One down and—

"Drop your weapon, Sir Ian. Or should I say Phantom?"

Marc's heart skipped a half beat, then he obediently dropped the Uzi as Ragno emerged from the tree, flanked by Giorgio and another man. Ragno held a .45 Magnum semiautomatic—no match for the Uzi, but that was on the ground at his feet. Ragno's two goons held AK-47's pointed at his bare chest.

He figured Tory needed another ten minutes to get away. He shifted his weight off his bad leg and waited, looking deceptively relaxed. When Ragno yelled for the rest of the men, Marc relaxed even more. Right now, all he could do was stall.

"You have proved a great inconvenience to my operation for many years," Ragno said coldly. The tips of his jutting ears were pink, and his uniform of U.S. Army fatigues looked ridiculously out of place on his bulky frame. "I should shoot you where you stand."

Nice to know that despite almost three years retirement they still missed him. Marc shrugged. "That's what I'd do if the tables were turned."

"You are very cocky for a man who might well bleed

to death," Ragno continued coldly. "Move over there." He indicated a stout tree. Marc dragged his game leg more than it warranted and shuffled in the general direction indicated.

How far had she gotten? Had she found the Vespa? Was she even now on her way to Lynx and safety? Christ, he hoped so. Because the alternative didn't bear contemplating.

"Tie him up." Ragno pulled a cloth out of his breast pocket and swiped it down his face as he watched his men dispassionately. "Test those bonds to make sure he can't get loose."

Two men, using thin wire, bound his hands and feet and stood at attention on either side of him. Marc leaned back against the knotty bark and tested the strength of his bonds. Tight and efficient. Shit. His vision was problematic. Now that he was standing still the blood ran unrelentingly into his eye, and he suspected a concussion was encroaching on his vision.

Damn and double damn.

"Before I kill you slowly, Phantom, you will tell me how many of your operatives know of my whereabouts." Ragno moved closer now that Marc was tied, still flanked by his small army.

"Operatives?" Marc mocked. "I don't know what you mean, old chap."

At a nod from Ragno, a fist landed on Marc's cheekbone, snapping his head back. Pain sliced through him and his stomach heaved as a series of blows landed—on the ribs a couple of times, then his face. Yeah, the guy was definitely a pro.

"What happened to your pal, Tweedledee?" Marc managed.

"I will ask the questions."

"Have at it. I'm a little tied up right now, so my time is all yours."

Ragno's eyes blazed. "You insolent fool. Answer me." He nodded to the guard on Marc's left. The man used his full strength to punch him in the solar plexus. Nothing like a fair division of labor. Marc's breath whooshed out of his lungs and he slumped back against the tree.

"I like games, Phantom. Very much." Ragno's breath stank as he pushed his face close to Marc's. "But I much prefer to play by my own rules. We enjoyed a little game with your slut this morning."

He stroked the side of his perspiring face with his handkerchief and smiled. "She's quite feisty, isn't she?" A nod of his head and the guard on his right punched Marc again. "She will screw anyone."

With effort, Marc kept his expression bland. Ragno returned to his original question. "How many of your people know of our whereabouts?"

"Let's just say that enough people know who and what you are to effectively eliminate you and your group." Marc managed to press his body upright against the tree, as he looked at Ragno contemptuously. "You don't for a moment think I'd come in alone, do you?"

"We will find them and eliminate every one."

"You and what army?" Marc sneered, blinking into the flashlights trained on his face. Where the hell was Tory? Safe? He strained to hear the *putt-putt* of the moped. Other than the wind ruffling the treetops and Ragno's uneven breathing, the forest was silent.

Ragno stepped closer still, and Marc wrinkled his nose at his stench. Christ, did this ass never take a bath? "I have an army," Ragno said smugly, fingering the collar of his fatigues.

"Yeah, the Salvation Army. Get real. What are you going to do? Talk us to death?"

Ragno snapped Marc's head back with an open-handed blow.

Hidden in the trees, Tory winced. All she could see was the back of Marc's head as it slammed to the side. But she could see Cristoph Ragno's face and torso quite clearly.

Sweat stung her eyes and she used her good arm to blot her face. The sound of the men's voices was almost obliterated by the thundering of her heart. Her hand, around the gun, felt slick and shaky. Oh, God, could she do it?

Not giving herself time to think, she edged closer. Something snapped under her left foot and she froze, her heart in her mouth. No one seemed to notice. She was as close as she dared. If she reached out her arm she could have touched Marc's shoulder. The gun suddenly seemed to weigh a ton. What did she know about guns, for heaven's sake? What if she shot Marc by mistake? The what-ifs buzzed in her head—but for only a second. Krista would have done it without blinking an eye.

Carefully Tory eased the gun firmly into her left hand, using the cast for balance, just as Marc had shown her. She turned on the laser and aimed. A red dot, the size of a dime, wavered on Ragno's shoulder. Then crawled, very, very slowly. Across his chest, his collar, his throat, and then paused. Tory held her breath trying to steady the beam.

How could the man not see the beam of red light? Tory moved the red beam unsteadily up the sweat glistening on Ragno's neck, up and up until it was aligned between his close-set eyes. For a moment she hesitated…

Then squeezed the trigger.

A second later she heard the pop. Then there was pandemonium. She refused to look as she ran from behind the cover of the trees, brandishing her gun.

She heard Marc's, "Hot damn!" but couldn't look at him. Suddenly calm, she lifted the weapon in steady hands and did a slow arc with the barrel.

Marc rubbed his face on his shoulder as Victoria came through the trees. The men stood stupefied, watching the small woman with the gun step into the clearing. Her hair swung wildly around her, the sleeves of the white silk blouse stuck out below the short sleeves of his black T-shirt, and there was a rip in the knee of her black slacks.

She looked magnificent.

She looked furious. "Drop your weapons," she snapped, the infrared dot moving from one to the other.

Marc's heart did a tango in his chest. Hell. They'd kill her before she could draw another breath. Straining at his bindings he prayed harder than he'd ever prayed in his life. Crazy woman, what the hell did she think these guys would do? Obey her?

Clearly surprised by her appearance, disheveled, one arm in a cast, bruises and lacerations on her face, the men took a nanosecond to train their weapons on her. The sound of a bullet being chambered sounded incredibly loud. The man hesitated. Probably never shot a woman at almost point-blank range before.

His hesitation cost him. Because Tory didn't hesitate. She pulled the trigger. Her bullet struck the man in the fleshy part of his thigh, and he went down screaming, trying to staunch the blood flow with both hands.

Every vestige of color drained from Tory's face, but she stared down the others. "Throw your guns over here."

Throw— Marc almost choked.

To his stunned amazement, they obeyed, tossing their weapons in Tory's general direction without mishap. Marc frowned, which hurt like hell. For these goons to be this compliant meant they had back-up. Somewhere. His eyes flickered to the surrounding trees, but he didn't see a sniper skulking in the undergrowth. Didn't mean there wasn't one.

He braced himself for the kill shot, even as he worked at his bindings.

"Get closer together," Tory told them, her tone tough and no nonsense. "Good. Now take down your pants." In case they didn't understand, she motioned her order with her free hand. After a blank few seconds they complied but, man, were they unhappy. Marc bit back a grin.

He didn't for a moment think these macho guys were going to let her get away with this, but for the moment it was damn funny seeing this petite woman holding off a gang of tangos.

The men unbuckled and unzipped, then dropped trow. Not a pretty sight, but an effective hobble.

"Now everyone lie face down—except you." Tory used the muzzle to indicate the man standing closest to Marc. *"Now."*

The men dropped to the ground.

Keeping her attention on the men lying face down in the dirt, Tory jerked her chin at the guy standing beside him. "Untie him."

As he felt the wire loosen, Marc brought his hands in front of him, rubbing his wrists. The man bent to free his feet. As soon as the bonds were loose, Marc kicked out with his good leg. The man flipped to the side and lay still on the ground next to his dead boss.

Tory hadn't turned the weapon off so the red dot made a small target on the man's chest.

"He's unconscious, sweetheart. Don't worry about this one."

Marc caught a movement out of the corner of his eye as someone tried to get up. "Victoria! Left!"

She raised the gun and pinned the other man in place. He dropped the pistol.

*"Hurry up."* Her voice rose. Marc noticed the fine tremor in her hands and hoped that the men didn't. He stepped over the unconscious man, his game leg numb, but he sure as hell wasn't going to wait around for Tory to be rushed by seven men. Limping, he came quickly to her side and relieved her of the weapon.

"Strip," he ordered the men on the ground. Much as he'd like to finish the job himself, he didn't have the time. He had to get Victoria to safety while he still could. By now Lynx would have called in the garbage detail. They'd remove the prisoners and interrogate them further. For now, his job was to secure them and get the hell out of there.

They looked at him blankly.

"Get naked, gentlemen, and don't mind the lady." Over his shoulder he said grimly, "Find the Uzi—I dropped it back over there." He wished his damned leg had stayed numb. He could feel warm blood seeping out of the wound.

She came back as the last man peeled off his underwear. She averted her eyes as Marc said, "Drop." They all fell in the dirt, facedown. "Grab their belts and whatever else you can find and start tying them up."

He knew he needed to get her moving so she wouldn't have time to think about what she'd just done. She was white-faced and glassy-eyed. Shock. But she did as he said, stripping belts from loops and shoelaces out of their shoes. He gave her top marks as she tied their hands and feet so that their legs were bent up at an unnatural angle, pointing at their heads.

"You're doing fine." He was going to pass out soon and he resisted with everything in him. She'd come this far. He needed at least to see her safely to the grotto.

He gave the seven trussed-up men one more glance, assessing their chances of breaking free, and took her arm.

After several yards he knew that there was no way that he was going to walk out of there on his own two feet. He'd lost too much blood, his vision was next to useless, and his leg wouldn't support his weight. He stopped to lean against a tree. "Princess, you have to get to the grotto and meet up with Lynx. Tell him where I am and he'll send someone back for me when you're safe."

She didn't bother answering him; she just pushed her shoulder under his arm and held tightly to his hand dangling between her breasts, forcing him to walk. The forest wasn't thick; it was more ornamental than wild. But the going was still rough. Thick shrubbery had grown between the trees, and the pathways were obliterated by years of debris, fallen leaves and branches.

It could have been hours but it was probably no more than forty minutes when Victoria slowed her pace. They had come to the road.

Marc was tortured by the fact that she'd practically carried him all this way. He could feel the sweat making her clothes stick to her slender back.

Tory's breathing was labored as she spoke—"I'll g-get…the Vespa." She moved from under his arm and steadied him against the side of a rusted tractor that had been abandoned at the side of the road. "I'll be right back."

"Tory…" But she didn't have time to listen to what he had to say. Every muscle in her body burned, she didn't want to pause long enough to think. If she paused for even a second, she would be lost. Her legs pumped faster as she rounded the barn and saw the scooter, partially hidden.

Marc tossed his good leg over the back of the seat as Victoria pulled up. *"Go,"* he said tersely, settling his hands in front of her to grip the pommel.

She went. The moped didn't go more than thirty-five

miles an hour, but they were moving in the right direction and hopefully had enough leeway for a clean getaway.

Tory angled her body to take a curve. This was suicide and she knew it. She was riding the unsteady scooter with a total disregard for their safety. The rearview mirror showed no headlights. But that could be as temporary as the next curve.

"Keep it steady," Marc warned, his hands holding on tightly to her hips.

The wind stung her cheeks and made her eyes water, but she concentrated on keeping them upright. The noise of the little moped was so loud. She wanted to look behind to see if they were being followed, but she didn't dare.

The moon came out from behind the clouds. It was almost as bright as daylight as they rounded the outside wall of Pavina, heading toward the beach and the grotto. The narrow wheels slithered on the cobblestones before hitting the tarred road.

The Vespa was unpredictable on rough roads and gravel. The last time Tory had attempted to ride one was on her first visit to Marezzo. That time she'd traveled at a sedate ten miles an hour, ignoring the impatient drivers that honked their horns at her. This time she pushed the little moped as fast as it would go.

She felt Marc's body slump, and she was terrified he'd fall off. She almost cried with relief when his arms tightened around her, and she took the dirt road toward the cliffs in a spray of gravel and dust.

The moped stopped in a shower of sand just as she felt his body slipping to the side. She managed to swing her arm back, supporting him while she kicked down the stand.

Using her body to prop him up she managed to swing her legs off the Vespa and looked down at him, biting her lip.

"Marc! Marc, up and at 'em. We have to get into the grotto so you can call Alex. Marc?" His head lolled on her chest. She pushed at him. "Marc, please. You have to wake up."

Glancing nervously over her shoulder, she saw the lights of a car coming down the main road toward them. Then she looked at the beach. The tide was out, the sand glistening in the moonlight was damp and the ocean was bright.

Tory scanned the horizon for the helicopter and Alex. The sky was empty. She bit her lip. Was she supposed to wait on the beach? Or had Marc and Alex devised some brilliant escape that they had forgotten to share with her?

"Marc, wake up!"

His eyes opened blearily as he stared up at her and then shook his head. "Lost too m-much blood. Go!"

"Oh, shut up!" Tory bit her lip. They moved slowly down the beach, her arms under his as she steered an erratic path down the hard-packed sand.

She had to take the risk of being spotted by staying close to the waterline where the sand was firmest. Nearer the cliff it was fine and dry and littered with rocks.

Her arms ached, as did her jaw from gritting her teeth, but they finally made it to the base of the grotto. Looking over her shoulder she saw the waves had washed out the tire tracks. Now all she had to do was get Marc up a mountain of rocks and rubble to the top. It was only thirty feet or so. She could do it. She had to.

IT WASN'T QUITE AS BAD as she'd expected. He was conscious enough to help, although sometimes it took a pinch or harsh words to get him moving. It was slow and torturous but they finally dragged themselves into the mouth of the cave.

Sprawled flat beside Marc, she struggled to draw breath into her heaving lungs. Sweat stung her eyes, but she didn't have time for that now.

She sat up and shook him. "Crawl over to where the bathrooms are," she instructed. He'd never make it back to camp and she didn't want to be trapped there if they were found. "Do you hear me Marc? Crawl…"

"I hear you, General." Marc struggled to sit up, a lopsided grin brightening his white face. "You are one hell of a woman, you know that?"

*Like Krista?* "How do we get hold of Alex?"

"Done. I called him back there before I found you. If…we're not back at the chopper site, he'll look for us here." His voice faded and his eyes drooped.

Tory shoved him, hard.

"I'm awake." He didn't sound it, but his voice was strong enough for her to know he wasn't going to pass out again for a while. "Got…to…get…bike…." He licked his dry lips as he rested his head against the rock wall. In the moonlight his face was a sickly gray.

"What?"

"They'll…see it. Moon too…bright."

She gave a silent groan. "I'll be right back."

The moped was on its side at the base of the rocks. Tory looked from it up the side of the cliff and down again, shaking her head. It had been all but impossible to push and prod Marc up that steep incline. How on earth was she going to pull the Vespa up there?

She looked around for a good hiding place, but there wasn't one. The rocks and boulders were large, but they were too close together. So she dragged the moped up and over the boulders, panting and swearing when she had the breath for it and mentally using all the cusswords she'd heard Marc use when she didn't.

She pulled it the last few feet and sank to the ground, her head on her knees. It would have been nice to take a rest, but unfortunately there wasn't time. Marc was back there and she needed to check the wound in his leg. God only knew what the next round held for them.

As she pushed the Vespa down the rocky corridor toward the lake, she prayed Alex would arrive with help soon. Marc had been right about one thing: she was no hero. Her brother couldn't arrive soon enough.

Pushing faster, she wheeled the scooter into the alcove that held the three Porta Potti cubicles, out of sight of the entrance.

Marc had propped himself against the far wall by the lake. "Lady, I have to say I'd have you on my side any day of the week." His voice sounded stronger but she ignored the useless compliment. If being by his side required that she got shot at, she would pass, thank you very much.

"I'm going to get the first aid kit. Is there anything else you need from camp?" She didn't like the gray color of his skin.

He closed his eyes at her militant tone and leaned his head back against the wall. "Bring the pack."

The camp was exactly as they'd left it. Tory bundled both survival blankets into the pack and looked around to see if anything else could be useful. The matches lay beside the small propane stove, and she shoved them into her breast pocket, then picked up the heavy pack, slinging it over her shoulder.

Marc looked slightly better when she returned.

She wrinkled her nose as he chewed a couple of dry ibuprofen—the water bottle and cups were back at the camp. His leg was a mess; drying blood had stuck the pant leg to his skin. "It's bleeding a lot, Marc."

Marc's lips were white. "Just put a pressure bandage on it to slow the bleeding… Shh!"

There was a scrape outside, as if a shoe had scuffed over stone. She and Marc froze, then Tory crawled silently to the opening into the main cavern. She glanced over her shoulder and raised four fingers.

Four men.

Marc swore, tightening his belt around his thigh, and motioned for her to stay where she was. She watched the men split up to circle the lake.

When she turned back, Marc was hobbling to his feet and doing something on the side of the moped. For one hysterical moment she thought he was going to ride the blasted thing down the side of the cliff.

He pulled the gas cylinder out of the A.L.I.C.E. pack.

"What are you doing?" she whispered.

"We're going to pour this on the lake." He hefted the spare can and indicated the moped. "Roll that over to the water."

Tory moved the Vespa out of its hiding place, and crouched down as low as she could between the shrubs and ferns. She followed Marc to the edge of the lake.

Marc unscrewed the cap and carefully poured the gasoline into the water.

"Get out of those pants and shoes," he whispered, his hand at his buttoned fly. "Leave on the T-shirt." His jeans dropped to the sandy floor a moment before hers did.

Marc's head disappeared around the edge of rock facing the lake. Seeing the back of his leg made bile rise in her throat. The bullet had passed all the way through. She avoided looking at the raw bloody mess. Crouching behind him, she settled her hand on his warm, bare shoulder.

One of the men had discovered their camp. He called to the others and they all disappeared behind the wall. Marc motioned her to move slowly behind him toward the lake.

His face glowed eerily in the diffused sapphire light of the water as he made room for her between the shrubs. The groundcover was cool and damp under her bare feet. Moisture from the ferns dripped on her cheek and she brushed it off impatiently. His leg was hot pressed up against hers. God that must hurt.

She tried to hold her breath for a moment to regulate it.

The four men came back around the rock wall, two

on either side of the lake. She pressed closer to Marc. "Now what?"

Keeping his eyes straight ahead, Marc said softly, "Now we wait until they get to...oh, about to that little tree over there—

*"Shit."* He patted his bare hip. "The matches are in the pack."

Tory wordlessly dug into her breast pocket and slapped the matches onto Marc's bare knee.

He looked startled for a moment and then cupped her face. "You are one sweetheart of a partner. Stick by me. I'll have you out of here in a flash." Dropping a quick kiss on her open mouth, he turned back to watch as the men got closer and closer.

"Why can't we just make a run for it?" Tory whispered desperately. She was getting a very bad feeling about this. The gasoline had spread in a thin oily film over the water. She rested her hand on Marc's arm. "We can slip by them, can't we?"

"We left the guns back there, Tory, and they'll see us as soon as we break cover. Besides, there are sure to be more of them waiting for us outside. We have to create a diversion. Improvise." He paused. "Listen."

The *chop-chop* of the helicopter was unmistakable. All four men paused for a fraction of a second, then moved faster, flanking the lake and moving swiftly toward them and the only exit.

He handed her a small cylinder and showed her how to clamp the mouthpiece so that she could breathe underwater. "Get ready." Marc struck a match. Flinging his arm up and over, he tossed it several yards out across the water. At the same time, he cried, "Jump!"

As they hit the water the flaming match ignited the gasoline. The sheet of fire spread rapidly, covering at least a third of the lake. Tory's head bobbed above the surface, eyes wide she watched the flames sweep toward them. Marc, grabbing her arm, pulled her inexorably toward the whirlpool.

Eyes burning from the thick smoke, she treaded water, feeling the pull of the whirlpool, then a steadying strength as Marc wrapped his arms tightly around her waist. She could hear the shouts of the men converging on the bank and then more running footsteps as they called for reinforcements. The cast was filled with water, the cotton padding swelled, getting as heavy as a stone and threatening to pull her under. It was like having a cinder block on her arm. Over the small mouth aerator she watched as the eye-level flames burned closer and closer. She put both arms around Marc's waist. He kicked his feet until they were swept into the vortex of churning water. The fire was spreading, sweeping the gasoline toward them in a blazing sheet of dancing orange and purple.

The voices got closer and louder. A gunshot reverberated against the cave walls, another splashed into the water close enough to spray her shoulder.

"Use the oxygen!" Marc inhaled deeply, his grip tightening. The sucking motion of the water caught her legs and pulled her under, and she squeezed her eyes shut as she held on tight.

For a split second she wondered how Marc was

going to hold that breath for however long it took to get through the forty-foot tunnel and out to the open sea. Then she could think of nothing at all.

Their descent was swift. The smooth stone walls of the tunnel were the only thing holding them right side up, as the force of the water pulled them downward in a violent spiral into the ocean. Marc's arms were wrenched away from her body as they scraped against the sandy bottom. The oxygen mouthpiece was wrenched from between her teeth by the force of the water. She had no idea which way was up.

Tory began to panic—her lungs felt as if they would burst. Forcing her eyes open, she allowed a little precious air to escape her lips. The bubbles rose slowly past her left shoulder, and she used her last ounce of strength to follow their ascent.

As soon as her face broke the surface, she gulped air into her starving lungs. High above came the unmistakable *whop-whop-whop* of helicopter blades beating the air. Spray flew off the surface as the movement churned up water, and white spray frothed in her face as she looked around frantically for Marc.

The pale gray of the sky blended into the dark gray ocean, making it hard to see. Swells lifted her, then dropped her down in a jumble of arms and legs.

*"Tory?"* She heard Marc roar her name, and choking and gagging, she fought the tossing of the waves, her hair blinding her as it slapped across her face.

He materialized behind her. His legs brushed hers as he trod water, holding her face above the churning sea.

Overhead, the blades of the chopper stirred up a

violent windstorm as it hovered closer to the water and lowered the rescue sling. The harness brushed the top of her head. Looking up, she saw the underside of the helicopter just thirty feet above them.

Marc snagged the harness before it sank beside her. Wedging his muscular thigh between her legs, he managed to secure the harness under her arms and keep her afloat at the same time.

The second he gave a thumbs-up she was lifted from the churning sea. As soon as Alex had hold of her, he sent the sling down for Marc. With Marc on board, her brother slammed the door shut and made his way to the controls up front. A few seconds later, Angelo knelt beside her, helping to support Marc as the chopper turned.

"*Buon giorno,* Signorina Victoria," Angelo said cheerfully as his large capable hands checked Marc's forehead. "Lots of blood from a head wound, not to worry. He will have—what you say? *Il mal di testa…*a little headache, that is all."

Tory collapsed. Alex would get them out of here. Back home. Back to her safe, predictable life. Back to being a coward and proud of it.

So why wasn't she happy?

## CHAPTER FOURTEEN

IT WAS EXACTLY SEVEN WEEKS, three days and five hours since the rescue. And Tory still hadn't got her life back the way it had been before Marezzo and Marc Savin. She knew she would never be the same again.

There wasn't a day that went by when she didn't think of Marc, long for him. According to Alex, Marc had recuperated and gone on to another assignment.

So he'd rejoined T-FLAC.

She was glad for him. He'd clearly missed his work.

She was terrified for him. She knew what that work entailed.

She became obsessed with watching the news. If there was a terrorist incident anywhere in the world she pictured Marc right there in the thick of things.

She was all right when she went to work every day at the auto-parts store. But in the quiet times at night, alone in her new apartment, she would think of him, dream of him, long for him.

Her breasts would ache and she would press her legs together. It took no effort at all to conjure up the memory of his callused hands. It took no effort at all to climax—alone and lonely. Before, she'd been alone, but never lonely.

She remembered every moment with Marc and steeled her heart against the poignant memories. Her rational mind knew that it would never have worked. Because even if he'd wanted her, really wanted her, there could be no future for them. She would never be okay with what he did for a living. Tory came home to her quiet apartment and hung her coat in the hall closet. The living room was frigid, but she tried to keep the heat down, striving to save as quickly as possible so that she could buy another condo. Maybe when she had a real home again she would feel more settled; at least that's what she kept telling herself. But she knew that wasn't true. She turned on some lights to dispel the gloom. Her grandmother's heavy furniture, taken out of storage, crowded the small space and suddenly she hated it. Hated the bulk and weight of the past hanging around her, suffocating her.

She vowed that as soon as she could afford to buy a home, she would get rid of all the bulky antiques and knickknacks, all the uncomfortable old furniture. Even if it meant sleeping on the floor. She had about six months to make it happen.

Resting her hand tenderly on her still-flat stomach, she went back to the kitchen to start dinner. She wasn't hungry, but the baby needed nourishment.

He was the best thing to come out of her adventure. Tory smiled sadly. The baby was the only thing that had prevented her from going into a dramatic Victorian decline.

Desultorily tossing a small salad and heating a can of soup, Tory took her meal back into the living room.

She hadn't heard from Alex in over a month. He was off on some mission, but she hadn't felt any stirring of fear. Since they could communicate in their own unique way, she knew that he was all right. At least physically.

He hadn't talked about the time he'd spent on Marezzo. Maybe he never would. He hadn't left her a letter this time. She doubted he'd ever do that again, either.

She'd talked herself blue, trying to persuade him to do something else, anything else. Perhaps, she thought without much hope, when he knew about the baby he would reconsider his dangerous lifestyle.

Tory picked at the salad and shook her head. Alex loved what he did just as much as Marc did. Neither man would ever give up vanquishing the bad guys—not for her, and not for the baby.

So she would keep the little guy a secret as long as she could. Then she would swear Alex to secrecy. Marc must never know.

Tory was pouring the rest of the soup down the sink when she heard a knock at the door. She groaned. It was that blasted man from upstairs who was always coming over on one pretext or another. He probably wanted to borrow sugar again. He'd never gotten the clue that she wasn't interested in going out with him.

She flung open the door, her expression militant. She was going to make sure that this time her neighbor took the hint.

It wasn't her neighbor.

"I see the cast is off." Marc's pale eyes darkened as they moved across her face like a caress. "May I come in?"

"Of…of course." Tory stepped back. He was all her wildest hopes and all her dreaded fears. "You're looking…well. How are you?"

"Fine. What are you doing here?" She tugged at the hem of her lavender wool jacket. Marc saw the telltale pulse in her throat above the delicate lace collar of her cream blouse. Her hair was in a neat coil on her neck, her tiny pearl earrings rivaling the sheen of her skin.

He closed his mind to the memories that had haunted him all these weeks. He remembered painfully what her satin skin looked like under that prim little suit, how her magnificent hair looked loose, and how it felt like a living flame when it touched his body.

His hands itched to reach out and touch her, instead he shoved them into his pockets as he remembered the sweet weight of her plump breasts in his hands.

He hadn't been able to erase the memory of her taste on his tongue or the scent of her from his mind.

He felt Tory's eyes on his back as he moved restlessly about the room, picking up a small china dog and putting it down again. His throat felt thick as he struggled—for the first time in his life—to put what he felt into words. Words that she would understand. Words that she would believe.

Tory watched him circle the small room like a caged panther. His limp was slight, but if she closed her eyes for a moment she could still see what that gunshot wound had looked like. She bit the inside of her lip to keep from crying out.

His black wool overcoat was open, showing the long

length of his legs, and she dragged her eyes away from the tight jeans.

Marc picked up a silver frame. "Your grandmother?"

Tory nodded. What was he doing here? She itched to touch the silky darkness of his hair where it lay against his collar. He had on a subtle, very masculine cologne; it teased her senses and made her long to bury her face against his neck.

She desperately wanted him to hold her.

Flicking on the lamp beside her, she sat on the over-stuffed sofa, pulling a needlepoint pillow into her lap to keep her hands busy.

The soft lamplight cast half his face in shadow, hiding the pewter of his eyes and delineating the rigid line of his mouth—the mouth that had brought her so much pleasure. He looked so good, his tall body softened by the open coat. But she remembered with aching clarity the feel of his hot, naked skin against hers.

The way his hands were stuffed into his front pockets pulled his jeans tight, and she had to swallow hard as she dragged her gaze upward to rest on his face.

His tanned skin in the middle of winter meant he'd been somewhere sunny. "You went back to Marezzo, didn't you?" She couldn't keep the accusatory note from creeping into her voice, her eyes skimming the small white scar on his forehead where he'd been branded by the bullet. She felt sick to her stomach.

"The job had to be finished." He circled the room again before coming to sit beside her.

She wanted to run her palms over his body to check

for any more damage. She pressed her hands between her body and the cushions on the sofa. It wasn't any of her business if he wanted to get shot. She dropped her eyes to her lap.

She started when she felt his finger under her chin. Her eyes wide, she drank in one last look at his beloved face. There were lines of strain beside his mouth, lines of exhaustion and a look of…longing? Which she didn't try to decipher. She closed her eyes.

"Will you look at me, Tory?"

She opened her eyes reluctantly, and he filled her whole vision. More powerful than any memory. It hurt, Lord, how it hurt. She bit her lip. She didn't want this last look to be blurred by tears.

"God, I missed you." His tone was husky as he cupped her face. She couldn't help the way her neck seemed to lose all strength as she leaned her head against his strong hand. His thumb stroked her cheek.

"I missed your snippy humor." His fingers slid to the lace collar at her throat. "I missed your sweet smile after we made love…." His hands opened the top two buttons of the silk blouse. Tory used a shaky hand to hold his marauding hands still against her pounding pulse.

"I missed the way this stubborn little chin tilts up…just so." His eyes were dead serious. "I missed that hidden fire that blazes out of control just for me."

"Don't," she said shakily, her heart throbbing. She knew that hot look. She'd dreamed of that look. But he wasn't for her. "Don't touch me. Please."

He didn't listen. He opened two more buttons until he got what he wanted. A vee of bare, silky skin. Parting the fabric, he reverently touched the gentle swell of her breasts above her very utilitarian white cotton bra. Tory shivered.

"You love me," he said with utter conviction, his eyes on her face. Blood drained from her head, leaving her weak and shaken. It was pointless trying to deny it.

"It doesn't matter." She pulled the throw pillow up against her chest, trapping his hand against her skin. "I'll get over it."

"I won't."

Her head shot up as she looked at him in disbelief. Surely he hadn't implied…?

"I love you, Victoria Jones."

"Since when?" She pushed his hands away and tried to do up buttons but they slipped between her nerveless fingers.

"Since I saw a sleepy woman spitting fire at me in my library that first day. Since I tasted these sweet lips, since I touched you, since…forever."

"That's sex, not love."

"That's what I thought at first, too. Marry me, princess. Marry me, and I'll show you how much I love you, in so many ways. You'll forget everything else."

"I can't. I'll never be able to forget what you do for a living." Tory said no even as she gave in to the temptation. She touched him back, drawing her fingers across the rough skin of his jaw to gently touch the scar on his forehead. "Every time you went away, I'd know… I can't live with that…." He took her hand, pressing a hard kiss into her palm. She curled her fingers inside his.

Her chest rose and fell. "I'd be terrified, especially

knowing what really happens in your job when you go on an assignment. I wouldn't ask you to change for me. And I don't think I can change enough for you."

She shuddered as he touched her fingers with his warm tongue. "I'm used to being safe, I like things predictable." She tried to pull her hand away from the erotic feel of his mouth. "I don't like to take chances, Marc. It frightens me." Her eyes filled as she looked at her lap. "I'm sorry, but I'm too old to change now."

Marc laughed softly. "You're definitely not a coward. You are the bravest woman I know."

"No, I'm not."

"How many women do you know who would save a man's life without a second thought?" He stroked her cheek with the back of his hand. "How many women do you know who would go through what you went through and not come back a basket case?"

"How do you know I didn't?"

"Because I know you, Victoria Jones. I know that you have the inner strength and the emotional fortitude to do what you have to do. You didn't fall apart." He dropped a tender kiss on her forehead. "And God only knows, you had every reason to come unglued on several occasions."

His lips moved to her temple, to touch the throb of her pulse.

"Life isn't as simple as debits and credits. There's no neat predictability, where all the columns are totaled and neatly balanced, like your ledgers. If life was as rigid as your accounting books, we would be bored to tears."

"Bored, but safe," she said as his lips skimmed her eyebrow. "I'd know where you were and when you'd be home."

Marc took her face between his hands. "I could get run over by a truck, sweetheart. Nothing is ever totally safe."

"But the law of averages is that much higher when you're being shot at." Her voice shook and she cupped his strong hands against her cheeks, holding them there tightly. "I've always hated what Alex did, and that was just a nebulous fear. Now I know and it's so much worse."

She felt his breath fan her face as he leaned down to silence her very effectively with his mouth. He tasted of mint and Marc—a flavor that she'd been yearning for for weeks. He drew her shoulders closer, deepening the kiss.

When he eventually broke away, he whispered against her skin, "We'll work this all out. I promise."

She'd seen him furiously angry, blindingly focused, playful, and tender, but she'd never seen such seriousness in all the time that she'd known him. There was even a small spark of…what? Fear? But that was impossible.

Marc had never been afraid of anything in his life. Had he?

"I had better tell you the whole story," he said. "After Krista…after Krista, I made myself believe that I was happier, safer alone."

"Oh, yes. Let's not forget the perfect Krista. Would you have—"

Marc gently placed a hand over her mouth. "Shh. Let me put Krista to rest once and for all. Tory, when I told you that Krista had died, I omitted telling you one of the most salient points. I was sleeping when an assassin broke into our room. I thought that Krista was beside me and I shot to kill. But the hit 'man' was Krista. I was the one who shot her."

"Oh, God. Marc…"

"When I turned on the light and saw her, I convinced myself that it had been a mistake. I frantically rushed her to the hospital. She was pregnant, Tory. I—"

"Don't do this to yourself. None of it matters now—"

"I went straight from Mexico to the ranch. And stayed there for two years. Alex was the one who told me that Krista had been the would-be assassin. He had proof." Marc pulled the leather tie out of his hair, scraping it back from his forehead with both hands. "Do you understand, Tory? I hid on my ranch for two years like some guilt-ridden fool, thinking that I had killed that innocent woman. That I had killed my child. For two goddamned years I'd allowed myself to wallow in guilt. I'd enjoyed my misery. And then your brother came and blew my life to hell with the truth."

Tory took his hands in hers. She was filled with pain. His pain.

"When I heard that Lynx had been killed, I really lost it. For the next six months I was worthless. I refused to go back into the field. I should have been with Lynx. I'd trained him, and he'd come to me for help. I refused him. The guilt and remorse I felt at his death incapacitated me. I fell apart. No man should collapse like a damned cream puff, but that's what I did.

"And then you came into my life and I wondered just what the hell I thought I could offer a woman like you. A burned-out mercenary? After I got back from Marezzo the second time and went to my ranch, I was missing you like hell and I finally realized that the solitude I had built around myself was nothing more than a jail. I might not deserve you, Tory, but I sure as hell need you. Tell me you missed me half as much as I missed you."

Missed him. Yearned for him, ached for him. Her voice was whisper soft. "Yes." She looked into his eyes. "Yes, I did. I'm so sorry that you were betrayed by someone you loved. I love you more than life. I would never betray you. But I have to be honest. Your job scares me. I know what it's like when you have to dodge bullets." She touched the scar on his forehead. "What if this had been two inches lower?"

"It wasn't."

"But it could have been."

"I retired," he said roughly. "I'm just a rancher that loves you. Come back to Brandon with me, Tory. I promise you a life filled with love and sunshine."

"I don't want to have you remind me for the rest of my life that it's because of me that you no longer do—"

"I'm not just doing this for you. After giving it a lot of thought, I've had enough. I need to move into the light with you. I can't live without you, sweetheart. Please, say yes."

He didn't give her a chance to answer. His mouth dropped to hers in a kiss so tender and poignant that it brought tears to her eyes. The familiar taste of him made her ache.

A shudder went through him as he pulled her closer, plucking the pins from her hair. His mouth moved in a slow dance across her face as he combed his fingers through her hair until it lay silky and loose down her back.

"Retired? Really?" she asked dreamily, feeling the delicious sensation as he lifted her hair at her nape.

"Really," he assured her. "I'd be thinking of you and then I'd get hard and I'd think to myself, 'Forget her.' But I never could." He smoothed the long hair over her shoulder, his eyes almost charcoal as they held the emerald of hers.

"I'm here to take you back with me. I can't live without you, Tory. Not for another day. I want you, need you to share all my tomorrows."

Tory stretched up to wrap her arms around his neck, his hair deliciously cool between her fingers. He deftly dispensed with the buttons on her blouse, tugging it out of the waistband, the hand behind her neck drawing her forward. He managed to part both blouse and jacket buttons, and then his fingers were at the front clasp of her bra, and she felt the cool air on her naked breasts.

Logic deserted her, falling away as his hand skimmed her breasts, weighing, teasing until she pressed closer.

His mouth against her throat was mobile, the hot, hard, questing pressure of his teeth making her shiver deliciously. He drew the fabric aside as he moved to take one aching peak into the cavern of his mouth.

He pressed her back against the soft pillows, his hard chest pinning her in place. His fingers slid beneath the heavy fabric of her skirt, up the length of her leg, smoothing along her thigh until he came to the moist heat of her through her panty hose.

His groan was muffled by the pressure of her mouth. He traced her lips and teeth with his tongue, as his hand slipped beneath the silky fabric to the smooth skin at her waist. Tory felt the withdrawal of her hose only dimly. Aching to be closer, she ripped at the buttons of his shirt.

Her hands were clumsy as she struggled to slide both his shirt and coat out of her way. It was impossible with their upper bodies melded together. Leaning her face against his chest, she felt his muffled, frustrated laughter.

With a low sound from the back of her throat, she lifted her face, starving for the taste of his lips again. It had been so long since she'd felt the fire of his touch. She couldn't get enough. As he loved her with his mouth, his palm covered her engorged nipple, rubbing and teasing until she shifted restlessly on the cushions. She looked up at him.

"Marc…"

"Tell me what you want, my love."

She saw the smoky pewter of his gaze, felt the strength in his arms as they wrapped around her. There was no doubting his love. She dropped her head to his naked chest. He smelled musky and sexy. "Anything. Everything. You," she whispered, her arms sliding up around his neck and holding him against her pounding heart.

He lifted his head, his hand cupping her stubborn little chin. "I love you more than life itself, princess. Come back with me. We'll raise cattle and babies…."

He buried his face in the fragrance of her hair, more afraid than he'd ever been in his life. Waiting for her answer was a thousand times worse than getting shot.

"You're mine," he said fiercely. "Tell me what you want from me, and if it's within my power I'll make sure you have it." His voice shook and he felt her arms come up to encircle his shoulders.

"You," she whispered brokenly against his forehead. "Just you. Safe and whole and…loving me. That's all I want."

"I'll give you all that and more." His mouth sealed hers with the vow. "We'll have the wedding at the ranch…."

He picked her up and carried her toward the bedroom. Tory kissed the corner of his mouth. "Yes…"

"I have a chauffeured limo waiting downstairs and the plane is fueled and ready…."

Her lips moved to his throat. "Fine."

Marc closed his eyes, his hands stroking down her back. He said with a mock sigh, "I guess the driver can wait."

Tory looked up into warm gray eyes. "The driver can come back tomorrow."

"Maybe the day after."

"Tomorrow," she said firmly, pulling him down onto the bed with her. "I'll be temporarily done with you by then. You'll need time to recuperate for the wedding."

He didn't…but she did her best.

# REQUEST YOUR
# FREE BOOKS!

## 2 FREE NOVELS
## FROM THE ROMANCE/SUSPENSE
## COLLECTION PLUS 2 FREE GIFTS!

**YES!** Please send me 2 FREE novels from the Romance/Suspense Collection and my 2 FREE gifts. After receiving them, if I don't wish to receive any more books, I can return the shipping statement marked "cancel." If I don't cancel, I will receive 4 brand-new novels every month and be billed just $5.49 per book in the U.S., or $5.99 per book in Canada, plus 25¢ shipping and handling per book plus applicable taxes, if any*. That's a savings of at least 20% off the cover price! I understand that accepting the 2 free books and gifts places me under no obligation to buy anything. I can always return a shipment and cancel at any time. Even if I never buy another book from the Reader Service, the two free books and gifts are mine to keep forever.

185 MDN EF5Y  385 MDN EF6C

| | | |
|---|---|---|
| Name | (PLEASE PRINT) | |
| Address | | Apt. # |
| City | State/Prov. | Zip/Postal Code |

Signature (if under 18, a parent or guardian must sign)

### Mail to **The Reader Service:**
**IN U.S.A.:** P.O. Box 1867, Buffalo, NY  14240-1867
**IN CANADA:** P.O. Box 609, Fort Erie, Ontario  L2A 5X3

Not valid to current subscribers to the Romance Collection,
the Suspense Collection or the Romance/Suspense Collection.

**Want to try two free books from another line?**
**Call 1-800-873-8635 or visit www.morefreebooks.com.**

\* Terms and prices subject to change without notice. NY residents add applicable sales tax. Canadian residents will be charged applicable provincial taxes and GST. This offer is limited to one order per household. All orders subject to approval. Credit or debit balances in a customer's account(s) may be offset by any other outstanding balance owed by or to the customer. Please allow 4 to 6 weeks for delivery.

**Your Privacy:** Harlequin is committed to protecting your privacy. Our Privacy Policy is available online at www.eHarlequin.com or upon request from the Reader Service. From time to time we make our lists of customers available to reputable firms who may have a product or service of interest to you. If you would prefer we not share your name and address, please check here. ☐